BLUE
WATCH

JOHN HARVEY

troika

Published by TROIKA

This edition first published 2019

Blue Watch was first published in France

in 2015 by Éditions SYROS

Troika Books Ltd

Well House, Green Lane, Ardleigh CO7 7PD, UK

www.troikabooks.com

A CIP catalogue record for this book is available

from the British Library

ISBN 978-1-909991-99-6

1 2 3 4 5 6 7 8 9 10

Printed in Poland

ONE

It was one of those nights when it seemed as if the whole of London was on fire.

What little cloud cover there'd been earlier had cleared and over two hundred enemy bombers had made their way across the Channel by moonlight, with close to a hundred fighters in support. At first it had seemed as if, yet again, their main target would be the docks either side of the Thames, but tonight the devastation spread far and wide.

In the north of the city, three or so miles from the centre, the streets were dark, the air thick with smoke and the smell of burning. Head down, Jack Riley swung his Fire Brigade messenger's bike hard left and right, avoiding the smouldering debris that lay scattered across the street. His objective was still some way off: a group of warehouses by the canal close to King's Cross station, where units from B District were fighting to bring a fierce blaze under control.

Like most nights since the Blitz had started, the phone lines were down and the only way of conveying messages securely from the Brigade control rooms to units in the field was by messenger.

On his first day the section leader at Kentish Town fire station, where Jack was based, had gripped his wrist and turned his arm sharply, pointing at the vein clearly visible beneath the skin.

'See this, Jack? This vein? That's you. Our lifeline. You and the other messengers, you're the ones who keep it flowing. Lose that and the whole service fails to function. We die. People die. You understand?'

Jack nodded. 'Yes, sir.'

People die. The words burned into his brain.

The officer's grip tightened. 'You won't let me down?'

'No, sir.'

'Good lad.'

Jack was shaking as he turned away.

That was two months ago. A lifetime, or so it seemed.

As Jack reached the crown of the road, pedalling fast, the loud roar of an explosion shook the air around him, lifting his bike off the ground and hurling him sideways, a flash of light outlining the skeletons of two towering iron gas holders, stark against the sky.

Shaken, he pushed himself up on to his hands and knees.

His regulation issue trousers were torn and there would be bruises, he knew, along with the grazes to his hands, but cuts and bruises were a given, a nuisance to be shrugged off and forgotten, along with the pain; what Jack was most concerned about was the state of his bike.

Fortunately, the damage was slight: the chain had come loose and the front wheel showed some faint sign of buckling, but nothing more. Chain quickly back in place, Jack pushed off and was away, head down into a hail of flying embers.

More than a dozen fire appliances – heavy units and trailer pumps for the most part – were ranged along the cobbled street that ran behind the threatened buildings. Jack lay his bike down and hurried between the maze of hosepipes criss-crossing the ground.

'Senior fire officer,' he called to the fireman on the nearest pump. 'Where'll I find him?'

The man pointed aloft, towards the turntable ladder that was reaching up towards the heart of the fire.

Jack swallowed hard and began to climb.

Above the first level the heat was intense. Smoke stung his eyes. The shouts of firemen rang around his ears.

'For Christ's sake hold that bloody hose steady!'

'Steady your bloody self!'

As Jack shifted his weight from one section to another, the ladder suddenly trembled, jolting him off balance, one foot perilously treading air some sixty feet above the ground.

'Easy, sonny,' a voice called out. 'No time to be practising your high wire act here.'

A hand reached out and pulled him to safety. Pale eyes peered out from a blackened face.

'What's the big idea?'

'A message for the senior fire officer, from control.'

'Round the other side of that girder. Him with the doodads on his helmet. And watch where you're putting your feet. That piece of floor's gonna go any minute.'

The fire officer took the envelope from Jack's hand, tore it open, scanned its contents, swore softly, and scribbled something on the reverse.

'Can I release at least two pumps to go down to St Katherine's Dock? No, I bloody can't, 'cause I need 'em here. But their need's greater than mine, poor bastards, so I'll have to agree. You'll find my leading fireman down below. Give him this. He'll know what to do.'

'Right, sir.'

Jack thrust the piece of paper into the pocket of his dark blue jacket and turned away.

'Hold on a sec. You're Ben Riley's boy, aren't you? Blue Watch?'

Jack nodded.

'He on duty tonight?'

'Yes, sir.'

'Good luck, then. The pair of you.'

More likely than not, Jack was thinking, his dad was one of those poor bastards the fire officer had mentioned, risking life and limb down on St Katherine's Dock. Shielding his face from the flying embers, he made his way down with extra care, hoping that his father was doing the same.

TWO

A year ago it had all been different. After the initial fears of imminent attack, the war – the real war – scarcely seemed to have started. Jack's father had just about finished his Auxiliary Fire Service training and his mother was still working as a secretary in the local council offices, not yet assigned to a government department that was so top secret, she couldn't tell even her own family where it was.

And Jack had still not been evacuated.

That is, he had. Just briefly, right after war had been declared. Packed off to an aunt who lived in Norfolk surrounded by cats and a small menagerie of stray animals she'd saved from being put down – two goats, a donkey and a three-legged dog amongst them. But when the promised bombs had failed to fall, like many others he'd returned home and back to his old school. Science, English, Geography, Arithmetic. Boring, safe and dull.

Where was all the excitement?

He would find out soon enough.

Wave after wave of German medium bombers began almost nightly attacks over London and the evacuation began in earnest.

His whole school moved out, lock, stock and barrel, to a small town in Cambridgeshire, some fifty miles away: teachers, pupils, everything. Cases were packed, labels attached; some of the older boys, like Jack, all of fifteen, were put in charge of the younger ones. Temporary homes had been arranged with local families, some in the town itself, others out in the surrounding countryside. Jack's was one of those.

'You'll have a great time,' his dad had said.

Jack hadn't looked convinced.

'Besides, it's for the best. Safer by half.'

'But what about you? You won't be safer. You'll be here.'

'That's different.'

'Why?'

'It just is.'

Jack had shaken his head and sighed: nice as his parents were, arguing with them, he'd learned, was useless, a waste of breath. Like parents everywhere, they knew best. Or thought they did.

'It's a working farm after all,' his mum had said with a hopeful smile. 'You'll be able to help with the animals and everything.'

Help with the animals proved right, if not quite in the way his parents had meant. Up at first light, feeding the pigs, collecting eggs, mucking out the stalls. Then there were potatoes to pull from the ground, earth to turn. The same every afternoon when they got back from school. Weekends, too. Slave labour, that's what it was. Granger, the farmer, red faced, rough shaven, forever needling, shouting, ordering them around. Not above giving them a kick up the backside or a clip round the ear if he thought they were being slow and wasting time.

His wife was no better. No sympathy from her. Just a bowl pushed in front of them at meal times, bread and soup more often than not, the bread hard and the soup watery. And little use complaining.

'Eat what you've got and be thankful. Don't you know there's a bloody war on?'

If ever Jack said anything to one of his teachers, the answer was always the same: stick it out, do your best, be thankful you're not still in London, hiding in shelters night after night, waiting for the all clear.

In his letters home, Jack made it seem as if

everything was okay. His parents had enough to worry about after all, the newspaper headlines forever trumpeting the worst:

LONDON'S BOMBING FIERCEST YET.
NEW EXPLOSIVE-AND-FIRE MISSILES
DROPPED.
DANGER OF INVASION STILL IMMINENT.

And all the while the anger at the way he and the others billeted at the farm were being treated festered inside him; anger waiting to burst, waiting for a moment of release.

When it came it was sudden, unthinking. One minute there was old man Granger's face looming over him – taunting, bullying, 'Get on with it, you lazy cockney bastard!' – and the next Jack was swinging a fist towards him, hard as he could. Smack into the centre of that leering face.

Already off balance, eyes splintering wide with surprise, the farmer stumbled back, legs giving way beneath him, his head landing with a crack against the rough edge of broken brick on the barn floor.

Jack's world stood still.

Silence, save for the breath and shuffle of animals in their stalls.

Granger lay, head awkward to one side, not moving. A little blood beginning to trickle from his nose. Eyes closed.

'Christ, Jack! What've you done?' Lennie, one of the other boys, his voice shrill from the doorway, pinched face pale with wonder. 'You've only bleedin' killed him!'

Down on one knee, Jack listened for a breath; searched for a pulse.

'Jack, you have. You've bloody killed him.'

Jack stood, uncertain. Head spinning. Heart pounding. Granger was still not moving, one leg twisted beneath him where he fell. Blood leaking now from the back of his head, bright and then darkening against the straw.

'Jack, you gotta go.'

He heard Granger's wife then, banging a wooden spoon against the rim of a saucepan, her voice impatient, demanding, calling them in for supper.

'Go!' Lennie shouted.

He didn't need another telling. As Mrs Granger neared the barn, he sprang past her, past her startled face and out across the yard, ducks and hens scattering in all directions. Granger's old bike was in its usual place, resting up against the water barrel by the back door.

One foot on the pedal and he was away, standing

clear of the saddle and urging every scrap of speed that he could. Out through the open gate and into the lane, the moon a faint blur overhead. Above the darkening hedgerows, an owl startled up, white-faced, from the branches of a tree.

Twelve miles to the nearest town, the nearest train station.

Twelve miles and then . . .

And then . . .

Jack slowed. Slowed and turned the bike around.

Sooner or later he would have to face the music: face up to the seriousness of what he had done.

Sooner was best.

THREE

The ambulance made its way carefully along the lane, headlights lowered so as not to attract any German planes that might be passing overhead.

Granger was sitting up now, propped against two bales of straw, holding a rinsed-out tea towel to the back of his head.

'Nasty cut that,' the ambulance driver said. 'Take a dozen stitches at least. Keep you in overnight, I dare say, just in case.'

In case of what, he didn't say.

The village bobby, Walter Ramsey, red of face after a laborious journey on his old rattletrap of a bike, took brief statements from both Grangers and from Jack himself, then spoke to Lennie and several of the other evacuees, who stood, huddled together, near the entrance to the barn.

Jack, the policeman said, had best go along with him.

'Lockin' up, Mister Ramsay,' Granger's wife urged, 'that's what he wants. And then the birch across his back.'

'I dare say,' Ramsay agreed wearily. 'Now if we can just borrow that bike for the lad, we'll be on our way.'

They followed the ambulance down the lane, Jack relieved to know the farmer's injuries were less serious than he'd feared, but worried about what would happen to him all the same. No way was he going to be allowed to get off scot-free.

'Where are you taking me?' he asked, once they were some distance from the farm.

'Back home with me, I reckon. Till morning.'

'Not jail then?'

'Not yet.'

They rode the rest of the way in silence.

The policeman's house was one of a small terrace towards the centre of the village, midway between the Grangers' farm and the town. As soon as it heard the gate, a dog inside began to bark.

'She'll not hurt you, shall you, Bess?' Ramsay said, opening the front door. 'Not without you giving her good reason.'

A black and white sheepdog cross, Bess circled round Jack suspiciously, snapping at his fingers when he reached out a cautious hand.

'Best leave her be till she knows you better. Not as that's going to happen.'

The inside of the house smelt stale and doggy, shorn of air.

'Sit yourself down,' Ramsay said, pointing towards an old armchair alongside the unlit fire.

Whistling, he left the room, leaving Jack to his own thoughts under the dog's watchful gaze. Some ten minutes or so later, still whistling, he was back, with a large mug of tea and a slice of toast and dripping for Jack and the same for himself. Bess sat at their feet, waiting for crusts.

'What do you think will happen?' Jack asked.

'To you? Not up to me. Lot depends on whether the Grangers decide to press charges.'

'You think they will?'

'Hard to say. But that regardless, the billeting officer'll have to be informed. School, too, I dare say. They'll have a view.'

'And my parents, will they have to be told?'

'What do you think?'

Eyes lowered, Jack bit down into his toast. What would be worse? His father's anger or his mother's shame and embarrassment?

Tea and toast finished, Ramsay stood, stretched and yawned. 'There's a bed upstairs, back of the house. You can have that.' His eyes shifted towards the settee beneath the window, several blankets stretched across. 'Since the missus died I've taken to sleeping down here with the dog.'

Jack woke early, uncertain where he was. When he eased back the curtains, the light to the east was pale and weak and a soft grey mist hovered above the fields. He could hear Ramsay moving around downstairs, Bess's hopeful bark, the opening and closing of doors.

He pulled on his clothes.

The smell of bacon frying drifted up the stairs.

'There's water in the outhouse,' Ramsay called. 'Soap and a flannel.'

Jack hurried down and, mumbling 'Good morning', found his way out back.

By the time he returned there were two well-crisped rashers waiting on a plate, mushrooms, egg and fried bread. A mug of tea. Jack's stomach rumbled appreciatively at the sight.

'Cost a fortune on the black market, that lot, down in the Smoke where you're from,' Ramsay said. 'Here in the country, we look after ourselves.'

Jack sat down and started to eat.

'Your old man,' Ramsay said. 'Off in the army, I suppose?'

Jack shook his head. 'Fire Brigade. He joined up soon as war was declared.'

Ramsay nodded. 'Better that than out in some bloody trench, up to his armpits in piss and shit. Mind you . . .' He prised a piece of bacon from between his teeth and offered it down to Bess. '. . . what you hear about all them bombs falling on the docks, night after bloody night, he'll be no safer there than having Jerry take potshots at him across the Maginot Line.'

Jack didn't know what the Maginot Line was, but he knew what the policeman said about the danger his dad was in night after night to be true. The tea tasted suddenly sour in this mouth.

'Soon as you've finished that,' Ramsay said, 'we'll be on our way. Billeting officer's expecting us by nine.'

Following the policeman's example, Jack wiped the last piece of fried bread around his plate.

Ramsay was quick to his feet. 'Best take this old scarf,' he said 'Nippy out there.'

Gratefully, Jack wound it round his neck, tucking the ends down into his coat. Stepping outside, he could see his breath on the air.

'Tell you this,' Ramsay said, 'if half of what I've heard about old Granger's true, it's a wonder someone didn't take a fist to him before now.'

* * *

They kept Jack waiting in a corridor of the Town Hall for more than an hour, before they finally ushered him into a chilly room where he was face to face with the billeting officer, a greying man with spectacles and a slight stammer, and two ladies from the voluntary evacuation committee.

'Well, young man. On the m-matter of last night's incident, what have you got to say for yourself?'

Jack explained what lay behind his sudden outburst of temper as best he could: the poor food, the long hours, the hard work, the farmer's constant bullying.

'I didn't mean to do it,' he said, finally. 'It just happened. I didn't mean to hit him. Not that hard.'

'Perhaps not,' said one of the ladies, not unkindly. 'But unfortunately that doesn't alter the fact that you did. And Mr Granger is in hospital because of it.'

They asked him to wait outside while they deliberated.

After twenty minutes, he was invited back.

'I'm afraid,' the billeting officer said, 'that your rash action leaves us with n-no alternative. You must return to London and your own family. We shall, of course, provide you with a travel voucher for your fare.'

'What about school, though?' Jack asked.

'I spoke with the headmaster earlier and he is firmly of the opinion that allowing you to remain unpunished would present a bad example to the other pupils. He doesn't want you back. I'm sorry.'

Less than an hour later, Jack was on a crowded train on its way to London, eager to be back home with his family, despite a sense of coming danger, and to be at the heart of where it was all happening. The heart of the war.

FOUR

'You daft young bugger,' his father said. 'What in God's name were you thinking of?'

Jack looked away.

Ben Riley finished buttoning his uniform tunic, then bent to wipe a scuff mark from one of his boots. 'There's a tin of soup in the cupboard if you're hungry. Your mum should be back around seven. Okay?'

'Okay.'

'And whatever you do, keep out of any more trouble.'

With that he was gone.

Left to his own devices, Jack couldn't believe how slowly the hands on the clock crawled round. A year or so ago, he would have rounded up some of his mates for a kickabout, or tried bunking in through the rear doors of the cinema when someone came out; but his friends were still in the country and now he was on his Jack Jones with nothing much to do and nowhere special to go.

He found one of his Biggles war books and tried to read but found his mind wandering before he got to the end of a page. Set against the real thing, the story didn't hold his attention in the way it had before. *FIGHTERS DESTROY NAZI RAIDERS* was the headline in the newspaper on the kitchen table.

In one of the fiercest air battles of the war so far, RAF fighters chased and harried German planes back across the Channel. No fewer than forty-five enemy aircraft were shot down, with seventeen of our own fighters being lost in the battle, the pilots of all but six ejecting safely.

Eleven men safe, Jack thought, doing the arithmetic in his head. Which meant that six of our fighter pilots were missing, wounded or dead.

There was nothing to say whether the German pilots had all gone down with their planes or if some had managed to bail out in time.

He pictured one of them parachuting into the sea

somewhere between England and France, struggling to free himself from the harness, then disappearing under the waves. Another landing somewhere on land, in what was to him a foreign country, possibly already wounded, searching desperately for somewhere to hide.

Just imagine, he thought, coming face to face with one of the enemy, wounded or not. Desperate, likely; dangerous. He'd heard rumours of groups of civilians dragging German airmen out of hiding and beating them half to death before turning them in.

Despite British successes, some enemy bombers were able to penetrate inland, causing considerable damage before turning for home. Casualties were described by official sources as moderate to light.

Jack pushed the paper aside.

If he didn't get out of the house soon he'd start climbing up the walls. Kicking the cat if there'd been a cat to kick.

Jack was surprised, walking north from the junction close to where he lived, and heading towards Parliament Hill Fields and Hampstead Heath, just how many houses had been badly bombed, some almost to smithereens. Empty doorways leading nowhere; shattered windows;

walls that supported their own weight and little more than a brace of sparrows, a passing pigeon. Mounds of broken bricks and mortar; shards of glass.

Casualties, Jack remembered from the paper, were moderate to light. What exactly did that mean? One family in hospital with serious injuries? Two? Three? More? How many missing? How many killed? He felt useless and alone.

Cutting through from bombsite to bombsite, a fine grey dust coated his shoes, clung in a thin film to his clothes, caught at the back of his throat and made him cough.

He was just clambering over what remained of someone's garden wall when the stone struck him on the shoulder hard and bounced away.

As he spun round, a second stone went flying past him, inches from his face, and then a third – not a stone this, more a chunk of broken brick – caught him square in the centre of his back.

Stumbling, for a moment losing his balance, Jack dropped on to one knee.

They showed themselves then, stepping out from behind the half-demolished buildings where they'd been hiding. Five of them. Scruffy clothes, pale threatening faces. Around his own age or older.

'Where d'you think you're goin'?'

The biggest stepped forward. A collarless shirt, torn

at the sleeve; trousers held up with a piece of string; what looked like old army boots on his feet. Down by his side he was holding a piece of iron pipe, eighteen inches long, that he was tapping lightly against his leg.

'Hear me, shitface?'

Jack shrugged, said nothing. If it came to making a dash for it, the best way, Jack thought, was back the way he'd come. As if reading his mind, one of boys moved swiftly, blocking his way, standing there with a sneer on his face, tossing a stone from hand to hand.

'This is our territ'ry, right? No one comes through here without our say-so. Anyone as does, they gotta pay.'

'I'm skint,' Jack said. 'See for yourself.' Pulling out his trouser pockets, he held the ends between finger and thumb. Nothing but fluff.

The leader's face twisted into a grin. 'Pay some other way, then, ain't yer?'

Jack watched as the length of pipe swung fast towards his head and, throwing up an arm to block it, he ducked inside and punched the youth in the stomach hard. The force of the blow was enough to stop him in his tracks, the pipe slipping through his hand down to the ground.

Jack braced himself and waited.

Fists flailing, the youth came back at him in a rush. Hands high, remembering the boxing lessons he'd had at school, Jack parried the first blow, swayed out of reach of the next, took the third on the shoulder, then, as the adrenaline rushed through him, he shot out a straight left that landed flush on his attacker's jaw and, closing fast, followed up with a short-arm jab to the nose.

With a yelp of pain, the youth faltered back, blood trickling through his fingers as his hand went to his face.

'Okay,' Jack said. 'You had enough?'

Slow to react before, the rest of the gang closed in fast. Jumping sideways, Jack tripped over an outflung leg and went headlong, sprawling across broken ground. Then they were on him, kicking and punching, cursing and swearing; they pummelled his face and arms, thumped into his ribs and thighs, fingers jabbing at his eyes. Each time he tried to push himself up, they dragged him back down.

Something – a brick or someone's boot – struck him hard across the top of his shoulders, hard against the bone, and pain lanced through him like a knife.

'Hey!' A shout came from the far side of the wall. 'Hey! What the bloody hell d'you think you're doing?'

The voice was loud, authoritative, strong enough to cut through the gang's angry braying.

'Cut that out. Now!'

One final kick into Jack's side and, grumbling and swearing beneath their breath, they stood away.

'Bunch of bloody bullies! Clear out of here now or I'll have the law on you.'

The man facing them was tall and wide, big enough to brook no argument, his dark blue overalls barely fastening round his considerable frame. A tin helmet sat firmly on his head, a large letter W, signifying Air Raid Warden, painted on the front.

'Sod off yourself, you fat bastard!' one of the gang shouted. 'Mind your own bleedin' business!'

But the warden stood his ground and grudgingly the gang shuffled back towards the nearest gap in the wall and, mouthing vain threats and promises, slunk out of sound and sight.

With a groan, Jack rolled over on to his back and eased himself round.

'Bunch of cowardly jackanapes!' the warden said, dismissively. 'Five against one, about their mark.'

Jack eased himself to his feet.

'Maxie Freeman,' the warden said, extending a hand. 'Looks as if I just turned up in time.'

'Yes, thanks.'

'You got a name?'

'Jack. Jack Riley.'

'Not Ben Riley's boy?'

'Yes.'

'Blue Watch, isn't he? Stationed up Chester Road. Yes, I know Ben. Heard him talk about you a few times, too. Thought you was off in the country somewhere, safe and sound?'

'Not any more.'

'Well, best get yourself off home and get them cuts seen to before they turn septic.' The warden laughed. 'Your old man claps eyes on you now, he'll reckon you've gone five rounds with Joe Louis.'

Jack grinned with sudden pride.

'And if you are going to stick around, make something useful of yourself. Not like that bunch of wastrels. Going to keep Hitler from getting his dirty paws on this country like he has everywhere else, we're going to need everyone to pull their weight.'

'I'd join up now if I could.'

'There's other things, you know. Messenger, for instance. Fire Brigade's crying out for them.'

'I thought they were all women on motorbikes. Least that's what my dad said.'

'Women, yes, and brave as any bloke you'll come across. Trouble is, more this goes on, there aren't enough of them. So they've started using messengers on push bikes – kids like you.'

For all Jack didn't like being called a kid, the idea of being a Fire Brigade messenger struck him as being great. The chance to get involved. Do something at last; something worthwhile. If only he could get his parents to agree.

FIVE

There was little chance, Jack thought, of his father being there when he got home, which was just as well. Much as he wanted to ask him about becoming a messenger, doing so while he was looking as if – what had the warden said? – he'd just gone five rounds with Joe Louis, wasn't such a great idea.

Best to bide his time.

Make himself look less like a walking accident.

What he hadn't banked on was his mum being back from work a good hour earlier than usual and sitting in the front room with her feet up, relaxing with a cup of tea, dance music playing quietly on the radio.

One look at Jack and she was on her way into

the kitchen, reaching for the bottle of Dettol in the cupboard under the sink.

There was a cut over Jack's left eye and a lump like a blackbird's egg at the back of his head. Where his trouser leg was torn, there was a deep graze oozing pus and blood.

'I don't imagine this was all a result of you tripping over your own feet?'

Despite himself, Jack smiled.

'Well, tell me about it in your own time. But I don't like you being in the wars. Not if it can be avoided. Now hold still, while I see to this.'

Jack gritted his teeth as his mum applied disinfectant to the open wound on his knee, then covered it with a fresh plaster.

'Right,' she said, when she'd finished patching him up. 'Beans on toast, what do you say?'

They sat at either end of the kitchen table and, gradually, Jack told her about both that afternoon's misadventure and what had happened, exactly, to cause him being sent back to London.

His mother listened with few interruptions, a nod of understanding here, a question there.

'We still don't know,' she said, 'if Mister Granger is going to go ahead and press charges or not.'

Jack breathed a sigh of relief.

'I might try and talk to someone up there tomorrow

and find out. Meantime, you look as if you could do with an early night. From the amount of cloud cover, I doubt if we're in for another raid, so we can sleep safe in our beds for once instead of the shelter. And no bombers means your dad might be back first thing in the morning.'

Not imagining he'd sleep well after what had happened, Jack slept the sleep of the dead.

When eventually he woke it was past ten and he could hear his parents arguing below. His father terse, angry, close to swearing; his mother calm but firm, refusing to be browbeaten or bullied into submission.

The voices rose to a crescendo and then suddenly stopped.

Silence.

Then the slamming of the front door.

Jack swung his legs round from the bed, a small jolt of pain from the back of his head as his feet touched the floor.

Downstairs, his mum was reading the paper, smoking a cigarette. In the background, the BBC newsreader was speaking of bombing raids as far afield as Bristol and Southampton.

'Your dad's gone back on shift.'

'I heard you arguing,' Jack said.

'Yes, I'm sorry about that.'

'What was it about?'

With a quick smile, his mum closed the paper at the

fold. 'Come on,' she said brightly, jumping to her feet. 'We're having breakfast out this morning, my treat.'

They went to a café close by the allotments on Parliament Hill Fields and sat at a table by the window, looking out over the rising grass towards the trees.

His mum ordered tea for herself, lemonade for Jack, toast for them both.

'I spoke to the billeting officer up in Cambridgeshire this morning. And the good news is the Grangers won't be pressing charges.'

Relief spread like sunshine across Jack's face.

'In fact, when they looked a little more closely into what had been going on at the farm, it sounds as if the Grangers came close to being prosecuted themselves. As it is, they'll be banned from taking any more evacuees.'

'Serves them right.'

'Exactly. What's not so brilliant, though, after what happened, the officer doesn't think it would be a good idea to have you back.'

'That's good, because I don't want to go back anyway.'

'There's always your Aunt Betty up in Norfolk, I suppose. I dare say she can find room for you again amongst all her waifs and strays.'

'Mum, no. I want to stay here.'

'It's not safe.'

'What about Nan and Grandad? If I've got to go

somewhere, why can't I stay with them?'

'Where they live, Whitechapel, it's even more dangerous than it is here. Every time there's a raid on the East End, I'm worried sick they're going to get hit.'

'Well if I can't go there, I'm staying here,' he said stubbornly. 'The war's here. You're here. I want to stay here.'

'Oh, Jack . . .'

'Stay here and do something to help. Be a bicycle messenger. You know, for the Fire Brigade.'

'Is that even possible?'

'I was talking to this Air Raid Warden about it yesterday. Maxie Freeman. He says it is.'

'It sounds dangerous.'

'Mum, everywhere's dangerous. You said so yourself. And they have these special yellow bikes, proper uniforms, tin hats, everything.'

His mother bit into a piece of toast and chewed thoughtfully, washing it down with a mouthful of tea. 'No promises, mind. But I'll talk to your dad about it, see what he says.'

'He'll say no.'

'Not necessarily. But now there's something else I need to talk to you about. Finish up and we'll take a turn around the hill.'

The trees, the horse chestnuts especially, were just

starting to change colour and lose their leaves. The air was bright and clear. Only a few stray clouds in the sky.

They sat on a bench and watched a kestrel hovering above the ground, its head still, only the wings moving, a blur catching at the light.

'Jack,' his mum said suddenly, breaking the silence. 'There's something I've got to tell you.'

Jack's stomach lurched. You're splitting up, he thought, you and dad. That's what you were arguing about this morning.

'This job of mine . . .'

'You've not been sacked?'

'No, no. It's just we're moving. I'm moving. Joining another department.'

'Promotion?'

'Sort of.'

'That's good, then.'

'Yes, it's good. And the work's probably more interesting. The thing is, it's not in London.'

'You're being evacuated.'

'In a way, I suppose, yes.'

'Where to?'

'That's it. I can't say.'

'What d'you mean?'

'I can't say. Where it is. It's secret.'

'Secret?'

'Yes.'

'You're going to be some kind of spy or something?'

She laughed. 'No. No. Nothing like that. It's just that some of the work that's done at . . . at this place is secret. That's why none of us working there can say where it is – or what exactly we do. Even if it's just typing or working a switchboard or, well, anything really. You've seen the posters, Jack. Careless talk costs lives.'

Jack nodded, his brain continuing to work overtime.

The kestrel had moved westward and was hovering over an area of taller grass, further away from the path.

'This place,' Jack asked, 'how far away is it?'

'Oh, not so very far.'

'Then you'll still be able to come home?'

'I expect so. Sometimes. Until I've started, I'm not really sure.'

'But weekends?'

'Jack . . .' She patted his hand. 'I've said, I'm not sure. Now come on, let's be getting back.'

As they got to their feet, the kestrel dropped almost faster than their eyes could follow and rose up again, a tiny shrew clasped in its beak, heading for a branch in the nearest tree.

'About being a messenger . . .' Jack said.

'I'll talk to your dad, don't worry. If I'm not going to be around so much, it might be good for you to have something to do. Something worthwhile, like you said.'

SIX

The smoke was thick, almost choking. Jack wrapped his scarf around the lower half of his face, rubbed the back of his hand across his eyes and peered into the murk. Making his way west through the maze of streets between King's Cross and Holborn, he'd found his path blocked time and again by burned-out vehicles and fallen buildings; near the corner of Russell Square, a bus had done battle with a burst water main and ended up leaning heavily to one side, one of its front wheels wedged into a deep hole beneath the road's surface.

Bobbie – short for Roberta – one of the two motorcycle despatch riders attached to the B District control centre in Kentish Town, had come off her bike that afternoon and was still getting patched up in

Casualty, leaving the section leader no choice but to ask Jack to pull an extra shift.

With little cloud cover to obstruct them or throw them off course, close to three hundred German bombers had made their way across the Channel, with a hundred Messerschmitt Bf109 fighters in support. RAF planes had gone up to intercept as usual, but despite intense fighting, the majority of the attackers had got through. Ten minutes over the city was all the time they had to unload their bombs before turning back and heading for their home bases in occupied France.

Ten minutes of devastation.

The night before over two hundred people had died, ordinary civilians for the most part, and more than twice that number had been seriously injured. And those numbers failed to include those whose bodies were still to be discovered, buried amongst the rubble.

Tonight could be as bad or worse.

A sudden flash of light across the sky revealed the colonnade at the front of the British Museum and Jack swung away to the left, turning right along Coptic Street and from there into the heart of the West End.

Some families from the East End, where, because of the docks, the worst of the German bombing had been concentrated, had taken to travelling up West in the evenings for safety and taking shelter in the basements of the big department stores before returning home the following morning.

'We're the ones gettin' it, night after night,' Jack had heard more than one East Ender say – his grandparents amongst them – while them up West get off scot-free.'

Scot-free no longer. For the last few nights, many of the big stores – Selfridges, Bourne and Hollingsworth, Peter Robinson's – had all been hit and tonight it looked like more of the same.

When he reached Oxford Circus, most of an entire block seemed to be ablaze, men from Blue Watch and several other parts of London doing their best to bring the fire under control and prevent it spreading even further. As Jack came to a halt he saw his father alongside Charlie Frost and a number of others, moving gradually forward through the scattered debris of concrete and glass and into the fire cordon, only to be forced back by the intensity of the flames.

The senior fire officer took the envelope from Jack's hand tiredly then handed it back.

'You open it, lad. Let me know the worst.'

A brace of incendiary bombs had landed close to the edge of Cavendish Square and the fire crew in attendance were having difficulty in keeping it under control. One of their pumps was out of action and a replacement had broken down on the way.

'You know where this is, the square?'

'Yes, sir. I think so.'

'You think or you know?'

'I know, sir.'

'Right. See that officer over there?' He pointed to a man leaning back for that moment against the base of a ladder, head down, helmet in hand. 'Tell him, twelve men, two pumps, one medium, one light, follow you. Now get!'

Jack scrambled away.

Within minutes they were around the square and into a street with shops on the ground floor and flats above: a chemist, a furrier's, a jeweller's, and, at the centre, a double-fronted dress shop with wedding gowns on display in its window. The fire seemed to have taken hold at either end of the terrace and be spreading steadily inwards, smoke billowing from the upper windows. For a moment, Jack thought he glimpsed his father climbing towards one of the far roofs, but he couldn't be sure.

'Here! Don't just bloody stand there! Gimme a hand with this.'

Behind Jack, one of the firemen from Blue Watch, a new man he didn't recognize, was playing out a hose from one of the pumps while another attached it to a vacant hydrant.

'I'll take the branch,' the fireman said, gripping the

business end close to the nozzle with his gloved hands. 'You keep the rest from getting fouled up and follow me.'

Blue and yellow flames leapt out of the shop front as they drew closer, and as Jack watched, the cream and white wedding dress at the front of the display shrivelled up before his eyes, disappearing into a cloud of ash and leaving the dummy it had been resting on blackened and burning.

The heat was intense.

Acrid smoke stung his eyes.

Two doors away to the left the front of the chemist's exploded outwards and the two firemen nearest to it were hurled back as glass splintered around them.

A sliver of blood lanced down Jack's cheek.

'Okay, son.' A gloved hand clamped down on Jack's shoulder. 'I'll take over from here.'

Grateful to be released from the heart of the danger, Jack relinquished his hold on the hose and backed away.

Too exhausted to climb back on his bike, he wheeled it on to the grass at the centre of the square, and sat with his back against a circle of iron railings guarding one of the trees.

Within minutes he was asleep.

By first light, when he awoke, the fire had been brought fully under control. The firemen still in attendance, his dad amongst them, were clearly exhausted, shattered, barely able to move one booted foot in front of the other. Though almost all of the fixtures and fittings had been lost, the framework of the shops had mostly been saved and even though a number of valuable items had been lost or destroyed, melted down, presumably, in the extreme heat, the jeweller's main safe had withstood the force of the fire. Those residents of the flats not already in shelters had been lifted to safety.

'All right,' the officer in charge said, addressing the men from his section. 'That's good work all round. A good night's work. But now let's get out of here and back to the station and, like the song says, no dilly-dallying on the way. Last team back gets to scrub down the heavy unit till it shines.'

Jack picked himself up and began the long ride home.

SEVEN

When Jack woke it was morning and he was in the house alone. His dad was not yet back and his mum still away at some secret destination with no sign of leave.

He missed her.

He understood all that stuff about careless talk, but surely she could have told her own family where she was?

Still – whatever she was doing, he was sure it was worthwhile. All part of the fight. And now he thought he ought to get his lazy self out of bed or his day off would be wasted. Not that he had any clear idea of what he was going to do.

But then, listening to the wireless while he was

eating his cornflakes, the newsreader talking about the fact the East End has been spared in the previous night's raids, he suddenly had both a purpose and a plan. He was going to get himself over to Whitechapel and see his mum's parents, his grandad and his nan. He hadn't seen them in ages. Not since he'd started as a messenger. And they were the only grandparents he had.

His dad's father and mother – Tom and Bess – he could scarcely remember. When he'd been just a toddler, not yet quite three, Tom Riley had been killed in an accident on the building site where he worked and his wife had caught pneumonia not so long after. There were photographs of them on the mantelpiece in the living room, alongside those of his mum's parents, Terry and Doris.

Jack worked the route out in his head. Down Tufnell Park Road to the Nag's Head, up towards the Angel and from there on to City Road and Commercial Street and he'd be as good as there.

A little more air in his rear tyre and he was on his way.

On City Road there were signs of successive raids: windows blown out, some partly covered over with planks of wood and lengths of linoleum; the brickwork at the side of one building almost completely stripped away; plaster and rubble everywhere; a washstand half filled with water where a starling was helping itself to a bath.

Closer to Whitechapel and the Royal London

Hospital, things looked even worse. The best part of a terrace demolished, roofs collapsed and gone. What had once been a small parade of shops – greengrocer, newsagent, butcher, hardware, boot and shoe repair – was now little more than a jumble of fallen masonry, tiles and glass. A set of spanners and a saw were just visible amongst the debris; screws and nails scattered like confetti; a boot mender's last; old newspapers shredded and torn, pages rising and falling with each turn of the wind.

At the corner of his grandparents' street, Jack held his breath, braced for the worst. But, some damage to the rooftops and chimney stacks aside, the terrace of small, flat-fronted houses had so far survived more or less unscathed.

His nan's face when she came to the door was a picture of astonishment transforming into delight.

'Tel! Tel! Come and look who's here!'

'Hello, boy!' his grandad, Terry, said, shuffling down the hall, hand outstretched. 'Not forgot us then?'

'Get yourself in here and take the weight off your feet,' his nan said, pointing towards the settee.

'Best bring that bike of yours in first,' his grandad said, 'or you'll get it nicked. Stick it out back, be safe there.'

'I'll get the kettle on,' his nan said. 'Make us all a nice cup of tea.'

It wasn't long before she was back in the front room with a tray: best china cups, teapot snug under woollen tea cosy, three slices of home-made Madeira cake on china plates.

Jack had been telling his grandad about his job as a Fire Brigade messenger and now his nan asked what had happened to cause him to leave the country and come back to London.

'Let the boy get something down him first, Doris,' his grandad said. 'He's come a long way.'

They looked on, expectantly, while he stirred his tea.

'Well,' Jack began, 'there was this farm where we were billeted, me and Lennie and a few of the others . . .'

While he was telling them his story, his grandparents hung on his every word and when he'd finished they looked at one another and shook their heads.

'Blokes like that farmer,' his grandad said, 'they ought to be locked up. Well out of there by the sound of it and good riddance.'

'Losing your temper though, Jack,' his nan said. 'Hitting him . . .'

'Shame he didn't hit him harder.'

'Terry, don't!'

'I know, I know. But bullies like that . . . It sticks in my gullet.'

'Never mind. He's here now, safe and sound, eh, Jack?'

Jack smiled. When he picked it up, the cake crumbled between finger and thumb and he only just managed to catch it on his plate.

Partly to cover his embarrassment, he asked about all the raids, night after night: weren't they scared?

'There's a shelter at the end of the street,' his nan said. 'Some nights we go there and if not, we go down the underground. Sleep on the platform. Got bunk beds down there now and everything. Mind you . . .' She wrinkled her nose. '. . . the stink's something awful.'

'Just two of them chemical toilets for all them people,' his grandad explained. 'Full to overflowin' by two in the morning. After that, well, it don't bear thinkin' about.'

'Let's not, then,' his nan said brightly. 'At least your mum's safe, wherever she is. Your poor dad, though, more dangerous what he's doing than being in the army. You know they used to call them cowards, some people, them like your dad as joined the fire service when war broke out. Cowards, I ask you.'

'Not any more,' his grandad said. 'Not since Jerry started coming over in earnest. They know better now. Either that or they've got their heads so far up their arse they can't see for shit.'

'Terry, don't! Not in front of the boy.'

But then she laughed and, after a moment, Jack joined in.

EIGHT

Not wanting to take the same route twice, Jack cut
through along Gray's Inn Road and from there down
York Way and on towards Kentish Town, Tufnell Park
and home. He was just turning into the high street
when a car went by him at speed, passing close enough
for him to wobble in its slipstream.

Just a hundred yards along the high street, the car
braked sharply and swerved up on to the pavement,
sending pedestrians scuttling for safety.

As Jack watched, it slewed to a halt close against
the front of one of the shops – Bryant's, the jewellers –
and a man's head and shoulders appeared through the
sunshine roof brandishing an iron bar, which he swung
with full force against the centre of the shop window.

For the merest of seconds, the plate glass seemed to hold before shattering across, the centre of the window falling forwards and breaking into fragments around the feet of the two men who had leaped from the car's interior. Ignoring the shop alarm they seized hold of the trays of necklaces and bracelets, rings and gold watches that had been on display, scooping them into big sacks – the alarm continuing to ring and people shouting, pointing, staring. No one yet daring to intervene.

When the robbers turned away, one of the bystanders, a man in a tweed jacket and a cloth cap, not young, tried to intercept them as they hurried back to the car and was punched in the face for his pains.

The driver, anxious, revved the engine and accelerated into action before the last man was properly on board, the door swinging wide and catching a carter's trolley as it headed back in the direction it had come, the direction in which Jack, straddling his bike, was standing.

Still not fully under control, the car seemed to be coming straight for him and at the last moment Jack jumped sideways, the car swerving in the other direction and scraping its wing mirror against the opposite wall before righting itself and speeding away.

Moments later the car was out of sight and Jack was rubbing his elbow from where he'd fallen, still not quite able to believe what he'd seen: a smash and grab in broad daylight. Yet, a little further along the street, the open, empty front of the jeweller's was all the proof that was needed, two members of its staff standing, dazed, on the pavement outside. And in the distance, the sound of a police car, coming ever closer.

At Holmes Road police station, everything was bustle and commotion. Telephones rang, voices were raised, footsteps, often hurried and heavy, echoed along corridors and down flights of stairs.

Along with a number of other potential witnesses, Jack's name and address had been taken and he'd been asked to come to the station for questioning.

The youngest, he was left to last. Stuck out in a corridor with nothing to look at other than some empty chairs and two walls that were blank save for an out-of-date calendar showing a view of Dover Castle.

'Just wait here,' the uniformed constable had said. 'Someone'll be with you shortly.'

That was almost an hour ago; more. The other witnesses had been and gone.

After another fifteen minutes Jack was convinced they had forgotten about him altogether. He was on the point of leaving when the same uniformed constable reappeared and led him to a room at the end of the corridor.

A knock, an encouraging hand at his back and he

was inside and face to face with a man his father's age or older, sitting slightly hunched behind his desk, tie askew.

The room struck Jack as cold, the air smelling oddly of something like the disinfectant his mum occasionally poured down the kitchen sink.

'Sorry if we've kept you hanging around, lad.'

'That's all right, sir, I . . .'

'Jack something, isn't it?'

'Riley. Jack Riley.'

The detective held out his hand. 'DS Reardon. Detective sergeant, that is. Local CID. And you're . . .' He glanced down at the sheaf of papers on his desk. 'You're a messenger, Fire Brigade, that right?'

'Yes, sir.'

'Well, sit yourself down. Let's get this done and have you back on duty soon as possible. Okay?'

Jack nodded.

'Just tell me exactly what you saw this afternoon. The more detailed the better.'

Jack told his story as clearly as possible, though lacking the degree of detail he was sure the detective would ideally have wanted. Two men in the front, one driving; two more in the back. Just shapes, little more. He remembered the colour of the car right enough, dark blue, and after looking at some photographs, agreed that it had probably been a Wolseley saloon.

He couldn't remember the number plate. At least, not exactly . . .

'There was a W. Maybe a 7, I don't know. It all happened so fast.'

'But a W?'

'Yes.'

'You're sure?'

"Ye . . . No. No, not really. Look, I'm sorry.'

Reardon barely disguised a sigh. 'How about the driver?'

'I don't know. Like I say, it was all quick. I was there with my bike and the next minute the car was coming right at me. It was all I could do to get out of the way.'

Reardon leaned towards him. 'Coming at you on purpose, is that what you're saying?'

'Not really, no. At least, I don't think so. I mean, why? Why would they? They were so desperate to get away the driver probably didn't even know I was there.'

'If they thought you might have got a good enough look to help put them behind bars, there's no knowing what they might do.'

'But I didn't.'

A quick half-smile. 'They don't know that, do they?'

'I suppose not.'

Jack shivered at the thought.

'And you're sure there's nothing about their faces,

the two up front especially – just think about it now – that sticks in your mind? Nothing out of the ordinary?'

'I don't think so, no. I'm sorry.'

'Oh, well. A pity, but there you go. Tell you what, though . . .' Turning, he pulled a large, leather-bound book down from the shelf behind him. '. . . just take a look through these before you go. Something might ring a bell, you never know.'

So saying, he left him to it.

Page after page of photographs – left profile, right profile, men looking straight ahead, unsmiling. Handsome men; ugly men; men with broken noses and cauliflower ears; men who looked angry, dangerous; men who looked, as his mum might have said, as if butter wouldn't melt in their mouths.

Not a single one that he clearly recognized. And he wasn't about to identify someone without being one hundred per cent sure.

What had the detective said about the gang and any witnesses? No knowing what they might do? He wasn't going to take that risk without good reason.

When Reardon returned and Jack told him he hadn't been able to pick anyone out, he didn't seem surprised. 'Not to worry, you did what you could.' A hand rested on Jack's shoulder. 'And now, you be careful out there on that bike of yours. Likelihood is, it's all going to get worse before it gets better.'

NINE

The detective sergeant wasn't wrong. An improvement in the weather led to the Luftwaffe doubling its efforts; raids both day and night now, with a consequent rise in the number of casualties. A hundred and fifty killed in Greater London, two hundred and fifty injured; in the following twenty-four hours, another two hundred were killed, with twice that number of injuries. After which, mercifully, conditions across the south-east changed: cloud cover night and day; persistent rain. London breathed easily if cautiously while other cities took their toll: Liverpool, Manchester, Sheffield, Birmingham.

Jack's mother phoned Chester Road fire station and left a message for his father with the switchboard: no promises, but there was a chance she might be able to get away for a weekend's leave. Just a day later she called back to say she was sorry but all leave had been cancelled. She hoped there would be another chance before too long.

Jack bit down into his lip and swore beneath his breath.

At the station itself, Ben Riley and the other crew took the opportunity to carry out necessary repairs to the equipment, practise drills. Jack returned from duty to an empty house. Made himself a cup of tea and a sandwich with bread well on its way to being stale and the last scrapings of jam from the pot.

Took them both into the front room.

One of his dad's favourite records was in its brown paper cover beside the wind-up gramophone. Fats Waller at the piano: 'Alligator Crawl'. Jack played it twice in succession before turning it over and listening to 'Viper's Drag'.

Leaning back in his chair, Jack closed his eyes. The slow rhythmic sound of the piano took him back to those evenings before the war when they would sit together, the three of them, his father tapping time on the arm of his chair, his mother darning a pair of socks or sewing up a tear in one of the shirts he wore for school.

When the music ended, Jack let the needle click for

some moments before lifting it clear.

On the table by the settee there was an old copy of *Picture Post* with a picture of Winston Churchill on the cover. Inside there were photographs of the German invasion of Belgium and Holland – whole streets on fire, building after building reduced to smithereens. A line of Nazi parachute troops dropping down from a cloudless sky.

'That's how they'll come when they invade,' Jack remembered old man Granger saying. 'Parachuting down. In disguise, some of 'em, too. Wearin' our uniforms instead of their own. Silent. You won't hear a thing.'

He wondered if that were true.

Wondered what Granger was doing now. Now that he had no more evacuees to work as slaves.

And Lennie, Jack thought? What had become of him? Lennie and all the other boys? He wondered if he'd ever see any of them again.

He turned the page of the magazine to pictures of families piling suitcases, blankets, and bits and pieces of furniture on to the backs of lorries; women pushing overloaded prams along cobbled streets. An old lady, bent almost double, her only possession, the small paper parcel she was holding in her hand.

All over the world, in Austria, Poland, and

Czechoslovakia, as well as in Belgium and Holland, streams of refugees have been set flowing by invasion.

Near the back there were photos of the Dutch Royal Family arriving in Britain, their children, two-and-a-half years and just nine months, being carried inside special gas-proof cradles.

With the fall of Holland, the war moves to within two hundred miles of Britain.

Jack looked at the date at the top of the page: May 25, 1940. That was not so many months ago. How much closer, he wondered, were the Germans now? How much closer to bombing them into submission? And all those refugees? Where were they? Some, he thought, might have made their way to England. If so, he wondered, would they have been made welcome? Found somewhere to live? Somewhere safe? Safe, at least, as he was himself.

Putting down the magazine, he opened the door into their small back garden where there was just room for their Anderson shelter, six feet long and high and four feet across. If the air raid sirens struck up later, that's where he would spend the night, restless on an old mattress and a random selection of cushions and pillows, never quite fully asleep, part of his mind on the alert for the sound of a bomb landing close by or the siren finally sounding the all clear.

Looking up into the sky, he could see the clouds were clearing, leaving a sliver of moon. Perhaps the Germans would be over later after all. But not yet. There was still time to get out for a walk; stretch his legs after being cooped up indoors.

Grabbing a torch from the kitchen table and a coat against the evening cold, he locked the back door and then the front behind him and pocketed the keys. Within fifteen minutes he was level with the allotments at the entrance to Parliament Hill Fields, continuing on past the café towards the hill itself. The path was for the most part deserted, a few couples walking slowly, speaking in lowered voices, the occasional firefly glow of a cigarette. In the distance, the insistent barking of a dog that ceased as suddenly as it had begun.

He stood for a while on the crest of the hill, looking out over the darkened silhouettes of the city, before turning away and beginning to walk slowly down the other side of the hill towards the ponds.

On the first pond, two swans stood out like sentinels by the far bank, pale in the gathering dark. Jack shivered. Coat or no coat, the cold was starting to bite into his shoulders.

Time to head for home.

As he reached the main road, the wail of the siren tore abruptly through the air and before he was much further along – a few hundred yards at most – he could hear the sound of anti-aircraft guns stuttering to life and the low roar of planes overhead.

Searchlights threaded the sky.

Half-walking, half-running, he hurried through the zigzag of streets towards home.

The next road he went into had been badly hit some nights before, a cluster of houses along one side little more now than broken shells. Not looking carefully enough where he was going, he tripped over a stray brick and went sprawling, hands barely breaking his fall, knees slamming down hard against the pavement.

No sooner was he back on his feet than he was thrown back again by the force of an explosion, the paving stones seeming to lift up beneath him and hurl him sideways against the rubble as dust and dirt showered over him.

Glass.

Fragments of brick.

There was blood on his face; the taste of it in his mouth.

Then someone shouting.

A boy's voice. 'Here! Over here!'

Wincing, he turned towards the sound. Fumbled in his pocket for the torch. Miraculously, it still worked, the beam picking out, low against the remains of a toppled rear wall, the quick, pale movement of an arm and then a face.

'Over here. Quick.'

Jack scrambled in the direction of the voice, crouching low.

'It's safe in here.'

Safe.

The face was still pale close to, the eyes anxious and dark.

Not a boy at all: a girl.

TEN

A girl.

Jack stared down into the darkness.

Hesitated.

And in that moment, the torch went out.

Behind him, another section of wall collapsed. Then another.

Still he hesitated.

'Suit yourself,' the girl said curtly and was gone.

Jack swallowed foul air, wiped the swirling dust from his eyes, and followed her down. The steps were narrow and uneven. Four, five, six, seven – when he next lowered his foot there was nothing.

'Be careful!'

As if he needed telling.

'Let yourself slide. Slowly. Slowly. That's it.'

Eventually, his feet touched solid ground.

'Now wait there. A moment. Just wait.'

He felt her moving past him, back towards the steps, then nimbly climbing; heard the scrape of some kind of board – he supposed that's what it was – being dragged across above his head, damping out the noise, shutting out the last faint residue of light.

A moment and she was back. Her arm brushing his as she went quickly past. His eyes struggling to make her out.

Then the quick scratch and flare of a match, and the hiss, like an intake of breath, of a candle wick catching fire. One and then another; stubs of wax set at different heights in different corners of the room.

Jack looked around.

They were in a low-ceilinged cellar running beneath the house, one part of which had clearly been used for storing coal. Now there were chairs: an old wicker one with a broken leg propped up on bricks; another with half of the rods at the back splintered away. In the far corner, close against the wall, there were blankets and a mattress. A small pile of clothes.

Someone's shelter; someone's home.

The girl was watching him all the while as he gazed around, taking it in. Cups with no handles. Plates. A knife. Half a loaf of bread. Milk bottles filled with water. A bucket with a lid. Sheets of paper on a trestle table; pencilled sketches of faces, flowers, trees. Books piled higgledy-piggledy on the floor.

'This is all yours?' Jack asked. 'All this stuff?'

She made a small movement with her shoulders, head a little to one side. 'Yes. Of course.'

'Where's it all from?'

'Some was already here. The rest I found laying around, dragged down.'

There was something about the way she spoke, the accent, something different – foreign – that he couldn't place.

'And you're what? Living here?'

'Why not?'

'How long for?'

'Two weeks, perhaps? Maybe not so much.'

'And it's just you? On your own?'

She shook her head.

Did that mean yes or no? He wasn't sure.

He looked at her properly for the first time. Her hair was cut short, well short of her shoulders, the ends jagged, as if she had cut it herself. Her neck was smooth and long; her eyes wide and dark and liquid in her face. Though she was dressed as a boy, it was the face that gave her away.

'Don't stare.'

'I'm sorry, I . . .' He began to blush.

'It's rude. Didn't your mother tell you?'

There it was, that accent again, more pronounced in some words, some sentences than others.

She sat down in the wicker chair, a quick gesture towards the other, as if inviting him to join her, but he remained standing. Above, muffled, the sounds of explosions were becoming more and more distant.

'Your head,' she said, pointing. 'You are bleeding.'

'It's nothing.' He touched his fingers to his forehead and they came away sticky with blood.

'You should wash it, I think.'

'It's nothing,' he said again.

She looked at him as if to say, your business, not mine.

Jack wondered if he should leave. If she wanted him to.

One of the stubs of candle guttered out.

'When this happened,' she said, 'the bomb, you were going home?'

Jack nodded.

'You are lucky then.'

'Your house, it was bombed?'

'Yes'

'And that's why you're here.'

'Of course.'

'But there must be somebody . . . somewhere you can stay . . .'

'Must?'

'Family somewhere . . .'

Something in her expression changed. 'I think you should go.'

'I'm sorry, I didn't mean . . .'

'The bombing is over. For now. They will be back, but not for a little time. It is safe to go.'

'Okay.'

At the foot of the steps, he looked around.

She was standing beside her chair. 'This time, look where you are going.'

He knew she was mocking him, just a little, but he didn't care.

Halfway up, he turned again.

'I don't know your name.'

'Lilith. And you?'

'Jack.'

Lilith, he thought, as he scrambled out on to the street, what kind of a name was that?

ELEVEN

Without meaning to, he caught himself thinking about her at odd moments through the following day. His mind otherwise empty as he carried out routine maintenance on his bike, readjusting the brake blocks, checking the pressure of the tyres.

Lilith.

Who was she? Jack wondered. Who was she really? And what was she doing, living in that cellar all alone.

His mind went back to those photographs of refugees, fleeing for safety. Was Lilith one of those? A refugee?

'Penny for your thoughts, Jack,' Rose, the taller of the two despatch riders, called across the yard.

'Dreaming about his girlfriend, I bet,' the other

rider, Bobbie, said with a smile.

'I haven't got a girlfriend,' Jack said, defensively, unable to prevent a blush from beginning to spread across his cheeks.

'Good-looking lad like you,' Rose said. 'Find that hard to believe.'

'Well, it's true.'

'You better watch out for Bobbie then. Now she knows you're not spoken for.'

Bobbie laughed and, lifting off her helmet, shook free a tumble of auburn hair.

Hunched over his bike, Jack went an even deeper shade of red.

Back at home, his father was pulling on his boots, getting ready to go back on duty, his dark blue tunic still unbuttoned. A cigarette, half smoked, was resting on the edge of the kitchen table; a mug of tea, half finished, a few stubborn crusts of stale toast.

'There's a tin of sardines in the cupboard, Jack. Beans, too, of course. Bread's seen better days, though, I'm afraid. Might want to give it a miss.'

'I'll sort myself out something, don't worry,' Jack said.

Sitting on one of the straight-backed chairs, he eased off his shoes.

'Blimey, Jack!' his father said with a grin, holding

his nose. 'I should get those feet of yours in a bowl of salt water before they walk off on their own.'

His father rinsed his mug under the tap, stubbed out his cigarette, fastened the remaining buttons on his tunic and set his peaked cap squarely on his head.

'Dad . . .'

'Yes?'

'You haven't heard anything else from Mum? 'Bout when she might be getting leave and that?'

'No, 'fraid not.'

'It's all right where she is though? I mean, she's not in any danger or anything?'

'I don't think so. No more than any of us. Less, perhaps.'

'You do know where she is, then?'

'No, Jack, I'm afraid I don't. I wish I did.'

'And you don't know what she's doing that's so secret?'

His father smiled. 'No, honest, I haven't a clue. And now I really do have to go.'

He reached for his helmet and haversack and turned towards the door.

'Dad . . .'

'What now?'

'Be careful, yeah?'

'Course.'

A moment later and he was gone.

Ignoring the sardines, Jack heated the beans on the stove and ate them straight from the pan with a wooden spoon.

Six o'clock. Not yet properly dark.

He washed his feet, changed his socks and his shirt, and let himself out of the house. Off to the east came the sound of anti-aircraft fire; several chattering volleys and then silence. A false alarm? Without telling himself where he was heading or why, he found himself at one end of the road where Lilith had come to his rescue five nights before.

Along one side of the street, the shell-like skeletons of buildings stood bare: doorways leading to rooms that were no longer there. A bathroom cabinet still fastened to the wall. A mirror that had cracked across, and by some odd circumstance not smashed to smithereens. What had once been a child's bedroom was little more than a blackened strip of wallpaper decorated with Mickey Mouse and Donald Duck.

He walked slowly now, not certain how far along the cellar had been. Then there it was – the right place, he was certain – an old door pulled across the entrance and weighted down heavily with bricks.

Jack kicked at the ground and walked on past, telling himself he didn't care if she were there or not.

Then there she was. A pale figure detaching itself

from the shadows on the far side of the street.

'Jack? It is you, isn't it?'

'Yes.'

'You weren't looking for me, were you?'

'No. No, not at all.'

'Just out walking?'

'Yes.'

'Going to the Heath, yes?'

'Yes.'

'Well, enjoy your walk.' She moved towards the cellar entrance. 'And if you ever did decide to pay me a visit, well, you know where I live.'

She shunted the door aside.

'Sometimes it's nice to have company, Jack. If only for a little while.'

A quick smile and she was gone from sight, leaving Jack staring at the scarred paintwork of the door she had pulled closed over her head. Wondering, as he slowly walked away, why he'd lied, what else he could have said. Glad that she couldn't see the disappointment in his eyes.

TWELVE

Mist, faint and damp, rose up from the river and combined with the lingering smoke from a hundred fires, making the task of navigating the damaged streets even more difficult than usual. Haphazard, half a ton of masonry lay strewn across the road, causing Jack to swerve wildly, narrowly avoiding colliding with a pram loaded high with a family's few remaining possessions, the woman pushing it clearly exhausted, barely able to set down one foot after another.

It had been a strange few days, fog over the coast inhibiting the German raiders, before clearing to leave bright autumnal skies and cloudless nights; the bombers coming over then in droves, their fighter escorts high and wide above them as they zeroed in.

Maidstone and Rochester on the Thames Estuary were badly hit, as were – yet again – the docks and the City of London itself. A bomb pierced the roof of St Paul's Cathedral, destroying the high altar, but leaving the main structure unharmed.

Phone lines were down for one night and much of the days either side, leaving all of B District's North Division – Islington, Euston, Holloway, Kentish Town – without direct communication.

An extra messenger was drafted in from another area but came to grief on only his second mission. Cycling at top speed along Upper Street, his front wheel got caught in a criss-cross of fire hoses, pitching him over the handlebars and on to the road, resulting in a fractured wrist, a badly bruised elbow and a cut needing a dozen stitches in his head.

Pitched yet again into a double shift, Jack was on his way back from guiding one of Blue Watch's trailer pumps to a warehouse fire off the Caledonian Road, when an Air Raid Warden stepped out from the ruins of a badly bombed house and waved him down.

The front of the building had collapsed inwards, one of the side walls the same; what had once been a roof was now scattered over the ground, covering a deep hole that had been gouged into the foundations. Broken brick on top of timber on top of broken tile.

'A minute ago,' the warden said, 'I heard someone

calling out. Least, I think I did. Down below there.'

Kneeling, Jack pressed his ear to the ground.

It was there, faint but unmistakeable.

A woman's voice?

A child's?

'Give us a hand with this,' the warden said, taking hold of one end of a heavy beam resting diagonally across the centre of the hole. Between them, they were able to lever it clear and begin the business of shifting the debris, opening up a way down below.

As Jack pulled away lath and plaster, he heard the voice again quite distinctly. One weak, despairing cry, then silence.

They set to work with even greater urgency until there was a way down into the blackness just wide enough for Jack to wriggle through.

'For God's sake, go careful, lad. Else you'll bring this whole bloody lot in on top of you.'

Burrowing like a mole, Jack clawed his way slowly down, using hands and elbows, pressing on his arms as he sought purchase, the earth seeming to fold about him, dirt falling across his eyes and into his ears.

'Hello!' he shouted, his voice muffled. 'Where are you? Answer me if you can.'

With a half-turn, he managed to squeeze both arms and then his shoulders lower still.

'Hello!'

No answer other than something moving faintly against the fingers of his outstretched hand.

Another hand, reaching for his own.

Fingers clutching his, clenching, holding fast.

Tightening his hold, Jack began to wriggle backwards, pulling the person with him; each movement slow and awkward, breathing more difficult now, the air thick and clotted with dust.

He kicked back with his legs once they were free and felt hands taking hold of his feet and ankles and pulling him out into the light of day.

At the last moment, the fingers clinging to his almost slipped away, but Jack managed to tighten his grasp before rolling free; turning, he saw the warden reach down and haul up a boy of little more than seven or eight years old, still wearing his pyjamas. Pulling him up and away from the hole in which he'd been buried since the previous night's raid.

Jack pushed himself to his feet and began to brush himself down. His jacket and trousers were covered in dust and dirt, the trousers snagged and torn in several places. His face and hands were black.

The boy was staring about himself in bewilderment, not able to understand fully what had happened, tears rolling soundlessly down his face.

And now others were arriving: several women from close by and an elderly man; another man, younger, in army uniform, cap in hand.

'Better give me your details, son,' the warden said, notebook in hand. 'I shall need them for my report. Some kind of commendation after this, I'd not be surprised.'

Jack didn't think that was likely.

Nor did he mind.

He'd done what there was to do and nothing more.

'Poor little blighter,' he heard one of the women say, nodding in the direction of the young boy, who was sitting on a pile of bricks with a blanket round his shoulders. 'Both his folk's goners. Brother, too. Whoever's gonna have the job of tellin' him, I'm glad it's not me.'

Jack righted his bike, swung a leg over the saddle, and was on his way. Faced with the emergency, the need to act and act fast, he'd gone ahead without thinking. But now . . . now he was beginning to realize the danger he had put himself in. And, more than that, what might have happened to the young boy if the warden had not heard his feeble cry for help. Trapped underground with no way of escape.

In his imagination, Jack saw Lilith sliding the heavy door over her head and disappearing, down into the dark. Alone.

'Sometimes it's nice to have company, Jack. If only for a little while.'

Why had he been so stubborn, so childish as to pretend then walk away?

THIRTEEN

Jack stretched and yawned and rubbed the remaining sleep from his eyes. His father had come home exhausted, crawled into the shelter, pulled off his rubber boots, and, within minutes, fallen asleep in his clothes. Now, when Jack entered the kitchen, he was standing, bright and cheerful, by the stove, whistling as he squeezed a last drop of tea from the pot.

'Day off for you today, isn't it? Thought you'd be getting a bit of extra kip while you had the chance. All those hours you've been putting in lately.'

'Something must've woke me,' Jack said, 'don't know what. Couldn't get back to sleep.'

'Maybe take a nap later, eh?'

'Yes, maybe.'

His father took a last slurp of tea and set the mug down in the sink. 'Leave you to wash up the breakfast things?'

'You're not back on duty this morning? I thought you had a rest day, too?'

'According to the rota, I did. According to the section leader, I'm manning the heavy pump, along of Charlie Frost.'

'Doesn't seem fair.'

'Tell that to Hitler, Goering and the rest. Where that lot are concerned, fair don't come into it.'

Jack cleared the tea leaves from the pot and rinsed it round before making a cup for himself. All the milk had gone, he'd have to drink it black. His mum used to like it like that, he remembered, with a slice of lemon.

'Getting proper sophisticated, aren't we?' his father had teased her the first time he'd seen her do it.

Smiling with her eyes, she'd poked her tongue out in return.

'If you do find yourself with nothing better to do today,' his father said, 'old Fred Campbell – you know, from down Huddleston – he was wondering if you might find a bit of time to help him out on his allotment. What with his fire watching and everything, he doesn't get time to do as much as he used to.'

'I'll see, Dad. No promises though, okay?'

'Fair enough.'

* * *

Fred Campbell had been a family friend for years. Friend as well as a sort of unpaid handyman. From when Jack was small he could remember him calling round at odd times to help set things to rights: a blockage under the sink that was proving too stubborn to shift; a window in need of replacement sash cords; advice on growing tomatoes. Not infrequently, he'd arrive on the doorstep flourishing a bucketload of manure collected from the road and some passing horse and cart. 'Just the stuff for the garden, Ben! Dig it in and smell the roses!'

Now, as Jack knew, he was an official fire watcher, stationed most evenings on the roof of an office block off Gray's Inn Road, his function during a raid to give warning of danger to those still working below and in the surrounding buildings.

Knocking on the door to number 19, Jack realized he'd never been inside the house before. No answer, he waited and knocked again. Still nothing and he was just turning away when he heard slow footsteps along the passage and then the sound of a bolt being drawn back, a lock turned.

'Now, lad, what's all the fuss?'

'Morning, Mr Campbell. My dad said you could do with a bit of help on the allotment and I wondered if this was a good time?'

'Good as any, I reckon. Matter of fact, I was just

fixing to go down there meself. Best come inside for a minute while I sort out the Thermos. Spot of something warm against the cold.'

He stood aside to let Jack in.

The lino in the hallway, Jack noticed, was splitting and curling up at the edges and the carpet was fraying badly on the stairs; the small kitchen, though, was surprisingly snug and warm, a fire burning on one side of the blackened kitchen range. Alongside plates and saucers on one of the shelves, stood a small framed photograph of a young man in army uniform, proud and smiling.

'Is that you, Mr Campbell?' Jack asked, pointing.

'No, that's my brother, Bill. Back in 1914. We'd just joined up, the pair of us. East Kent Regiment. The Buffs.'

He lifted the photo down. 'This'd've been taken not so long before we set sail for Le Havre. The war to end all wars, that's what they said.' He made a quick, bitter sound in his throat. 'The Great War, so called. Ten million dead, and now we're having to go through it all again. Didn't end bloody anything.'

'And your brother . . .?'

'You've heard of Passchendaele?'

Jack shook his head.

'Like Hell but worse. I got through it, Bill didn't. Stayed there in the mud.'

He set the picture back in place.

'Now let's get this Thermos fixed. Hot tea and a drop of this to top it off.' He took a small bottle of brandy from the kitchen drawer and unscrewed the top. 'Don't worry, just enough to give it some snap. Not enough to get you drunk, big lad like you.'

They worked on the allotment for several hours, stopping every so often to take a break, an opportunity for Fred Campbell to stretch his aching back and for them both to have a swig of tea. The brandy made it taste strange, not altogether unpleasant; more like medicine, Jack thought, than anything else. He kept wanting to ask about the war, what it had been like, but fought shy, thinking Campbell might not want to be reminded of what had happened to his brother. And then, when he was about to pluck up courage, Campbell was already on the move.

'Come on, Jack. Can't chuck in the towel now.'

There was plenty to do and no mistake. Another crop of potatoes to be harvested and carrots, too; beans and a few lingering green tomatoes. Jack shook the excess soil from the potatoes, scraping away the more stubborn bits before putting them in a hessian sack, prior to being stored in the shed. Fallen leaves he collected with a rake and dragged them over to the far corner to moulder under a square of staked-out chicken wire.

And there was digging, always digging. The ground that had been made vacant turned over and spread with manure, horse droppings some of it, collected from the road when the milk cart had gone past.

'Leave that in large clumps there, Jack. No call to break it up any smaller than it is. The worms'll do that for us, you'll see.'

When, finally, the flask was empty and Mr Campbell was showing every sign of being done for the day, Jack finally got his chance.

'The war – when you were over there, all that time, in France, fighting the Germans – what was it like?'

Fred Campbell looked at him keenly for several long moments before answering.

'Sometimes it wasn't too bad. You were with your pals, good pals, you'd have a laugh and a smoke. But most of the time, like I said before, it was like Hell. That trench you dug there, for instance – imagine them by the dozen, each one six foot or more deep and stretched out as far as your eye could see.

'You're standing there, or crouched down more like, up to your knees in piss and shit, waiting for the next Jerry shell to come over or the next attack, and all the while there's rats swimming round you, gnawing at your ankles, and you're thinking any bloody second I'm going to get blown to kingdom come.

'And if that don't happen, we're going to get the

order to go over the top, and chances are I'll end up face down in the mud, or skewered on barbed wire with a bayonet through my guts. That's what it was like.'

He hefted a sack of vegetables up on to his shoulder.

'Now let's get home and out of harm's way, before the bloody bombing starts.'

FOURTEEN

There was little or no respite: the Luftwaffe testing the RAF's air defences in the south-east at the same time as spreading their targets west and north. Southampton, Plymouth, Liverpool, Manchester, Coventry, Wolverhampton.

In London, St. Matthews Hospital on City Road, a former workhouse with 600 beds, suffered a direct hit. Several of the buildings close to St Paul's went up in flames, but the cathedral itself was virtually unscarred.

Jack had been at the site of the hospital fire, abandoning his bike to join the frantic effort to carry stretcher after stretcher of seriously sick or injured patients from the building before the walls caved in, taking the ward floors with them. Ambulances came from other parts of London to ferry away those who had survived. Many did not.

Still Jack worked on until, muscles aching, his legs buckled beneath him and he pitched forward, exhausted, amongst the dead and the dying.

One of the ambulance men helped him to his feet and out of harm's way.

'You take it easy, lad. You've done your bit. And more besides. We'll handle it from here.'

Some fifteen minutes later, Jack was sitting on the kerb, head in hands, when a hand gripped his shoulder.

'You okay, son?'

It was his father. His face streaked with black; his uniform dark with smuts and soot.

'Yes. Yes, I'm fine.'

The hand moved to tousle his hair. 'You did good work there. Saved lives. I saw you.'

'You did? How come?'

Turning, his father pointed back towards what remained of the hospital roof, outlined against the violet darkness of the sky. 'I saw you from up there. Pointed you out to Charlie. Made me feel real proud.'

Jack grinned with pleasure and his father smiled back, eyes bright in his smoke-smeared face. 'I've got another twenty-four hours of this before I come off watch. I'll see you sometime tomorrow.'

Jack pushed himself up on his feet. It seemed right to shake his father's hand.

'Take care, Dad, yeah?'

'You, too.'

Jack watched as his father walked determinedly back towards the fire cordon, tightening the strap on his steel helmet as he went.

Pride works both ways, Jack thought.

Later, making his way wearily home, that strange time between day and night, the light gradually fading, Jack was just crossing the bridge over the canal on York Way, when a lorry turned sharply out of the side road that came up from the station, sending his bike into a wobble that nearly sent him tumbling.

'Hey!' he shouted, righting the bike and bringing it back under control. 'Watch what you're doing!'

The lorry carried on its way, the driver oblivious.

Not so much further along, Jack knew, there were traffic lights, with any luck about to turn red. Up from the saddle, he gave chase, intent on giving the driver a piece of his mind.

The lorry a hundred and fifty yards ahead of him.

A hundred.

Head down over the handlebars Jack increased his speed.

Through the gloom he could see the traffic lights begin to change.

All of a sudden a saloon car raced past him, overtaking in the opposite lane then swerving in front of him with a squeal of brakes that came close to unseating him for the second time in as many minutes.

As the lights turned red and the lorry's rear brake lights came on in response, the car swung out wide again and came to a screeching halt broadside in front of the lorry, blocking its path.

Jack veered quickly off to the side, towards a patch of ground at the entrance to a small block of flats; laying his bike down, he crawled up to the low wall at the pavement's edge.

Two men had jumped from the car and were shouting up at the driver in his cab, banging on his door. When he tried to put the lorry into reverse, one of them pulled an iron bar from inside his coat and smashed the windscreen into a web of shattered glass.

Then, as Jack watched, another man, tall, more smartly dressed than the others, dark overcoat and homburg hat, leather gloves, got out of the car, and, not hurrying, walked to the driver's cab and wrenched open the door. What he said, Jack couldn't hear, but whatever it was, it had the desired effect.

As the man in the hat stepped back the driver climbed down cautiously from his cab. As soon as he did one of the others pushed back hard against the side of the lorry, spun him round and clubbed him over the back of the head with a sickening crack.

Jack caught his breath.

With a laugh, the man in the homburg strolled back towards the car while the others half-carried, half-dragged the lorry driver to the opposite pavement and began tying his legs together at the ankles, his hands behind his back.

Remembering his interview with the police detective after the smash and grab raid, Jack shifted his position so as to have a better view of the car. The colour was dark: a darkish green. Bottle green, is that what he'd heard his mum call it? Yes, bottle green. And the car itself – a long front and a curved back. Wasn't it an Austin, like the one his dad's friends had? He thought it was.

The registration, though . . . from that angle, in that light, he could hardly make out the number plate at all.

The car horn sounded impatiently.

Now or never, Jack thought and, crouching low, ran towards the end of the wall to get a better look at the number plate.

TLR?

ILR?

748?

743?

TLR 743??

One of the men climbed up into the lorry, fired the ignition, and within moments both car and lorry had disappeared from sight.

What seemed to have been happening while time had stretched or stopped altogether had taken no more than a matter of minutes. Jack reclaimed his bike and crossed the street to help the lorry driver and then contact the police.

FIFTEEN

Once Jack had reported what he'd seen, Detective Sergeant Reardon arranged for him to come back into the police station with his father the following day, his dad in his uniform, having begged an hour off duty.

The room seemed colder than before; the scent of disinfectant, if that's what it was, stronger than ever.

'Drains,' Reardon explained, seeing Ben Riley sniffing the air. 'Right outside this window. Forever blocking up. Bugger to clear.'

Leaning forward across his desk, he shook the hand of first father and then son. His tie, Jack noticed, was even more askew, the knot almost out of sight behind one wing of his collar.

'He did well, your boy,' Reardon said, with a nod

in Jack's direction. 'Kept his nerve. Kept his eyes open when it mattered.'

'He's not a bad lad,' Ben Riley acknowledged. 'Head on his shoulders.'

Jack felt himself starting to blush.

'Gets himself in the thick of it, though, doesn't he?' Reardon said. 'First the smash and grab and then this. Not thinking of joining us when you're a bit older, are you, Jack?'

'Not really. No. That is, well, I've never really thought . . .'

'Time enough for that,' his dad said. 'No need to rush.'

'That's true. All in good time.' Reardon sat back down, indicating they should do the same. 'Since Jack's given us this useful information, got himself involved without really wanting to, I thought a bit of background might be useful.' Reardon leaned back in his chair. 'How much d'you know, either of you, about London gangs? Criminal gangs?'

'Not much, I suppose,' Ben Riley said. 'What I read in the papers from time to time, that's all.'

Jack simply shook his head.

'They've always been around, one way and another, some more dangerous that others. The Sabini family from Little Italy, for instance, seriously nasty bastards – excuse my French – and the Whites from round King's Cross not much better. Then you've got the

Hackney Mob, the Elephant Boys, and closer to home, the Heavy Mob, Kentish Town's finest.'

Father and son exchanged glances. Close to home indeed.

'Like I say, they've always been there, but now, with the war, the Blitz, all the confusion everywhere and the extra cover they get from the blackout, they're getting bolder than ever. Downright cocky. You've seen it for yourself, Jack: smash and grab on that jeweller's shop in broad daylight.'

'Pulling that kind of stunt,' Ben Riley said, 'they must know there's a risk they'll get caught?'

'Risk, yes. But while there's money to be made, big money, they don't care. And the real risk, of course, is sooner or later someone – some innocent bystander, maybe – sooner or later someone's going to get seriously hurt. Killed even.'

'That last hijack, for instance . . .' Looking at Jack now. '. . . all it would have taken was another swing with that iron bar, or for that driver to have had a soft skull and once he'd gone down he wouldn't have been getting up.'

He paused a moment to let that sink in.

'What were they after, anyway?' Ben Riley asked. 'Something valuable, surely? To be worth all that.'

'Cigarettes. That's what. Cartons of cigarettes. Even though they're not officially rationed, as you might have noticed they're in short supply. A load such as that lorry was carrying would be worth three or four times on the black market what any regular bloke'd expect to pay over the counter. Which, from the criminals' point of view, makes it well worthwhile.'

'And was it this Kentish Town gang then? The . . . what was it . . . Heavy Mob?' Jack asked.

'It's possible. Their territory, just about. Though the King's Cross boys might have something to say about that. Thing about the Heavy Mob, though, from what we hear, what we can tell, they're a bit, you might say, rudderless right now.'

'Rudderless? How d'you mean?'

'They used to be run by this Billy Hill. You've heard of him, maybe?'

Both Ben and Jack shook their heads.

'Smart as a whip, Billy. Flash, too. I'd have a drink with him from time to time, one of the boozers around. My line of work, it happens. Bull and Gate, maybe, Bull and Last. Billy dropping little hints all the time, about what he'd been up to. All a bit of a game to him.' Reardon's face broke into a grin. 'Till he finally overstretched himself a few months back, got himself nabbed in the middle of Bond Street: smash and grab gone wrong. Billy's inside now, enjoying two years at His Majesty's Pleasure.'

'Good thing,' Ben said.

'Yes and no. Without Billy, what you've got is a loose bunch of wastrels and chancers not above losing their heads. Taking foolish chances. And desperate enough if they're cornered to shoot first and ask questions later.'

'They're armed?' Ben Riley said, alarmed.

Reardon nodded. 'Deserters, some of them. And when those blokes go on the run you can be sure they take their weapons with them.'

Ben Riley's face showed a mixture of dismay and disgust.

'I'll tell you one thing, though,' Reardon said. 'What interested me about this man Jack described as orchestrating the hijack – smartly dressed, homburg hat – that profile very much resembles a certain Vincent Crella. Until recently known to be up in Glasgow and mixing with some decidedly shady types. Razor gangs and the rest. When things got too hot for him up there he went to ground. To all intents and purposes, disappeared. Rumour had it he was down here in the Smoke, looking for a place to hang that hat of his. But until now, we didn't know where.'

'And you think that was him? This Crella?'

'Could well be. Billy Hill going inside wouldn't have escaped his notice. Crella might've taken it into his mind those were a pair of shoes he could fill. And this cigarette business, that might just have been his calling card.'

'What I don't understand,' Jack said, 'is if you know that much, why don't you just arrest him?'

Reardon smiled.

'Not that easy, I'm afraid, son. We pick him up now and almost as soon as we've got the cuffs on him, some clever lawyer will have him back out again. So what we do: we watch, we wait, pool all the intelligence together and then when the time is right, we jump. See him put away in Pentonville till the war's over and things have had a chance to get back to normal.'

With that, Reardon got to his feet.

'Thanks to both of you for coming in. After what Jack'd done, I thought you ought to be brought into the picture. And Jack . . .'

'Yes?'

'If you do keep up this habit of yours, of running into nasty situations, well, keep your head down and your eyes open. Just like before.'

Jack grinned. 'I'll do my best.'

They were almost home, just coming up to the Boston pub, and about to turn right down Tufnell Park Road, when Jack found himself suddenly face to face with Lilith, balancing a cardboard box on her shoulder and walking directly towards them.

Lilith, with her short hair even shorter than when he'd seen her before, and wearing what looked more like boy's clothes – boots, a grubby pair of dark trousers, a v-necked sweater with the sleeves rolled up to the elbows and a collarless shirt beneath.

'Jack! Jack, it's you,' she said, her voice rising. 'I thought one day I must bump into you again.'

Jack wanted the ground to open and swallow him up.

'And you,' Lilith went on regardless, 'you must be Jack's father. So pleased to meet you.'

Ben Riley shook the girl's proffered hand, her grip small but strong.

'And you are?' he asked.

'Lilith. I am Lilith.'

'Well, Lilith, it's good to meet you. I see you know Jack here already.'

'Yes. We first met not so very long ago, didn't we, Jack? There was a raid and Jack took shelter with me for a little while. Isn't that so, Jack?'

'Hmm,' Ben Riley said, amused at his son's embarrassment 'You must have forgotten to tell me about that, eh, Jack? Slipped your mind.'

Jack thought he wanted to die.

'Tell you what,' his father said, 'why don't you give Lilith a hand with that box of hers? Help take it wherever it's going. Looks pretty heavy to me.'

'It's all right, really,' Lilith said, 'I can manage.'

'Nonsense. He'd love to help, wouldn't you, Jack?'

Jack thought he might scream.

'Just don't be too late back, okay?'

And with that his father strode away, leaving the pair of them together.

Lileth's face creased into a smile.

'What have you got in there anyway?' Jack asked.

'Tins of soup. Dented and bashed around but still okay.'

'Give it here then.' Jack reached out his hands. 'We can take it in turns.'

Lilith grinned. 'Thank you, Jack. You are true English gentleman.'

SIXTEEN

Across the centre of the cellar floor there was a length of carpet, patterned orange and brown and quite badly burned at the edges, that Jack didn't remember being there before. And, behind the trestle table, a small wooden cupboard, the kind that his parents used to have beside their bed, with a chipped china vase on top and a few scarlet flowers poking out hopefully.

'Where d'you get all this?' Jack asked. 'This new stuff?'

Lilith shrugged. 'Around. Here and there.'

'Scavenging, isn't that what it's called?'

'Is it?'

'I think so. It was in this story I read once at school.

About pirates. Well, sort of. Sort of pirates. These boys, three of them, they've been press ganged . . .'

'Press what?'

'Press ganged. You know, kidnapped and taken out to sea. And the ship, the pirate ship, gets wrecked in this storm. Smashed up on the rocks, and they swim to shore. It's an island, an uninhabited island – at least, that's what they think at first – and what they do is swim back out to the wreck and take what they can of the supplies. Scavenge. That's what it means.'

'I see. Thank you. I did not know this word. Scavenge, yes, that is what I do.' She was smiling, smiling with her eyes. 'These boys,' she said, 'I suppose on this island, they find buried treasure, yes?'

'Not on the island. Down in the ship's hold.'

'And they are all boys, this adventure? No girls?'

He realized she was mocking him, just a little, like before. 'It's a story for boys,' he said, defensively. 'That's what it is. There are different stories for girls.'

'Yes. I have read these stories. *Little Women*, I think. *What Katy Did. What Katy Did Next.*' She gave a dismissive shake of the head. 'I did not much like this Katy.'

She raised both hands up in front of her daintily and assumed a voice more exaggeratedly girlish than her own. 'I mean to be beautiful, of course,' she mimicked, 'and good if I can. And I'd like to have a large house and a splendiferous garden and do something grand. That is Katy.'

Jack laughed.

'I would like to have a grand house, too, perhaps some day,' Lilith said, back in her own voice, 'but for now this will have to do.'

'It's okay,' Jack said. 'I like it. I like it here.'

'Well, if I were Katy, I should most probably invite you to have tea. Would you like tea, Jack?'

'Yeh. Yes, thanks.'

'Then please, be seated. Be my guest. I'm afraid it takes rather a long time.'

In one corner there was a makeshift grate with a pile of sticks and some rolled-up balls of newspaper and Jack watched as Lilith struck a match to begin a small fire, blowing on the embers until they caught, gradually adding more wood and a few pieces of coal. Emptying water from a jug into a battered and blackened old kettle, she set that directly on to the fire, wedging it into place to prevent it from overbalancing.

Quite proudly, she fetched a white teapot with a chipped lid from inside the new cupboard and with it a screwed-up packet of Typhoo tea.

'I suppose that's all scavenged, too?' Jack said.

'Of course.'

'How far do you have to go? Looking for things?'

'Oh, sometimes not so far. Sometimes Highgate,

Highgate New Town I think it's called, up the hill from here. Sometimes Holloway; sometimes Kentish Town.'

'That's where I was born,' Jack said, 'Kentish Town. We moved up here to Tufnell Park when I was really little. One, two – something like that. How about you?'

'What?'

'Where were you born?'

The merest flicker of a pause. 'Berlin.'

Jack blinked. 'But you're not . . .'

'Not what, Jack? What's the matter, you can't say the word?'

'It's not that, it's just . . .'

'Not German, that's what you mean.'

'Yes. But you can't be. Surely?'

'Why ever not?'

'You don't look . . .'

'I don't look German? What do you expect, Jack? I should be wearing a swastika, waving a Nazi flag? Have funny little moustache here, perhaps?' She pressed her little finger against her upper lip. 'Walk like this?' Pushing past him, arms swinging straight and high, she began goose-stepping around the cellar. 'Is this what you want?'

When she turned back towards him, Jack looked for the smile on her face, looking to see if she were joking. She was not joking.

'I'm sorry,' he said. 'I didn't . . . I don't understand.'

* * *

The milk had gone sour, curdled, so they drank the tea black, Jack spooning in as much sugar as it seemed polite to take, while Lilith reminded him of his mother by adding a slice of sorry-looking lemon the greengrocer had thrown out with his rubbish. There were broken biscuits and a piece of stale fruit cake, which Lilith cut carefully into four small squares.

'My family,' she said, 'we are Jews. You know what it means to be a Jew?'

Jack didn't know how to answer. He had some vague notion of someone foreign, old men with beards dressed all in black, those little black caps on the backs of their heads. Mean, that's what it meant, too, didn't it? Mean. Tight with money. At the sweet shop where they used to stop on the way to school, if ever anyone refused to pay his share, the others would shout, 'Jew! You Jew!'

'I don't know,' Jack said eventually. 'I'm not sure.'

'In Germany,' Lilith said, 'since Hitler, it means you are treated like vermin, the lowest of the low. We are not allowed to go to normal schools. On buses, in trains, even benches in the park, we have to sit on special seats, away from the rest. Everywhere we are bullied. Spat at in the street. My brother, he was beaten up – not once, many times – the last time so bad we had to take him to hospital and at the hospital they turned him away.'

'But why?'

'Why? For being a Jew. It is enough.'

'I don't understand.'

Lilith sipped at her tea; it was hot, still too hot to swallow.

'My father,' she said, 'he taught at the university – English, English Literature, Shakespeare – he was professor. One day, when he arrived to give lecture, he was told, sorry, he could not teach there no more. When he tried to protest, go to his class, they send for the security police, throw him out on the street.'

'I'm sorry.'

'Now it is worse, they burn our houses, burn our shops. Our synagogues. My father, this professor, he was forced to scrub clean the pavements, scrub on his hands and knees. Again, he protest. This is not right. The next day, they come for him, the SS, take him away. A year now, almost. We have not seen him since. No letter, nothing. We have no idea where he is, if he is alive or maybe already dead.'

Jack could only shake his head.

Lilith's eyes were closed. The cup shook a little in her hand.

Carefully, Jack took it from her, set it down. Waited until she felt okay to carry on, her voice quieter, a little less certain than before.

'My uncle, he said he could smuggle us out of the

country, my mother, my brother, my little sister and myself.'

Jack recalled the photographs he had seen of refugees desperately searching for another home.

'We would come here to England, he said, to friends. My aunt, she would come also. At the last minute, my mother refused to go, she said she would not leave without my father, not knowing where he was, when he might come home. My brother stayed with her. So it was just my aunt, my sister and me. At first we lived with a family in Whitechapel – you know this?'

'Whitechapel, yes. It's where my nan and grandad live, more or less.'

She nodded. 'Then some other people took us in. Not everyone was welcoming to refugees, Jews especially. But they were kind. This was after the bombing had started, the air raids. Most nights, we would go to the shelter, not so far away, but it was so crowded, so many people, and it smelled, smelled terrible, so sometimes we would stay in the house. Sit, all huddled together, in the space below the stairs.

'And this one night – I'd had an argument with my aunt – something foolish, I can't remember – and I went off to the shelter on my own. I thought I was being so big and brave, grown up.'

For a moment, she looked away, tears springing to her eyes.

'In the morning, when I went back after the all clear, the house had been bombed. The houses both sides as well. A direct hit, the warden said. My sister – I saw her doll, this doll she always held on to when she was frightened; it had blue eyes and long, fair hair. It was there, just sticking out above these fallen bricks, all broken . . . And, Jack, ever since then, I have felt guilty to be still alive.'

As she cried, Jack reached slowly out and took hold of both her hands and, though she closed her eyes as if to stem the tears, it was a long time before she pulled her hands away.

SEVENTEEN

After leaving Lilith in the cellar, Jack spent the night in the Anderson shelter, and, try as he might, he found it difficult to sleep. The image of Lilith's sister's doll kept playing continuously, like a piece of trapped film, inside his head. The more he tried to shake it free, the more it became mixed up with what he remembered of searching frantically to rescue the little boy trapped beneath his bombed-out house. Only this time, when he reached down towards the boy to pull him clear, the boy's arm came away, doll like, in his hand.

Jack sat up in a sweat.

A cold, shivering sweat.

Pulling on his clothes, he stepped outside.

A crescent of moon sat sharp in the sky.

Stars.

The orange glow of burning rising up, distant, from the city.

Acrid smoke, drifting on the wind.

Back indoors, Jack filled the kettle and set it to boil. Shook the last remaining cornflakes into a bowl, sprinkled on sugar, added a splash of milk, careful to save enough for his tea.

Not for the first time, he wished his mother were there, someone he could safely talk to about the feelings racing round in his head, someone who would understand.

In an hour, though, maybe a little more, his father should be coming off watch. He'd walk up the hill to the sub-station at Chester Road and meet him; he didn't think his dad would mind. He'd been there enough times carrying messages and the other men were used to seeing him around. Reg Simpson, the leading fireman, dark-haired, strict-looking and strong-sounding, but a good bloke, his father assured him, his bark worse than his bite. And Charlie Frost, his dad's best mate, not so much taller than Jack himself, with a round, red face and a cockney accent sharp enough to slice bread.

Charlie had grown up in the East End, not so many streets away from Jack's grandparents. He'd moved to North London after he left school, starting work as a trainee butcher at a branch of Sainsbury's in Camden Town. Jack's father he'd got to know on the terraces at White Hart Lane, watching Spurs the season they finished fifth in the Second Division, 1937–38; then that summer they'd played in the same Sunday League cricket team at Regent's Park, Charlie a fearless wicketkeeper, often standing up to the fastest of bowlers, Ben Riley a steadfast opening bat, wearing down the opposition with the straightest of defences, before slashing the ball spectacularly through the covers or driving it back over the bowler's head. Saturday nights they would often share a pint or two at the Boston or the Bull and Gate.

By the time Jack reached Chester Road that morning, Blue Watch were already back, Reg Simpson supervising essential repairs to one of the heavy trailer pumps in the yard; most of the men stripped down to their shirts and braces and winding down with a mug of tea after another hard night's work, smoke still threaded through their hair and etched into their faces.

Inside, in what, until the outbreak of war, had been a junior school hall, a few had begun a game of darts, a shout going up as one man followed up a bull's eye with a double top. Charlie Frost and his dad were at opposite ends of the table tennis table when Jack entered, Charlie sending down smash after smash, all of which Ben Riley clipped calmly back until his opponent, frustrated, swung wildly, the bat flying out of his hand in one direction and the ball sailing high into the air in the other and then rebounding from the ceiling.

Laughing, Jack clapped his hands over his ears. Most of the curses that came from Charlie's mouth weren't new to him, even if he'd never heard them in exactly that order.

'You didn't hear any of that, son,' Ben Riley said, unable to suppress a grin.

'No, dad. Not a word.'

'Come on over here. Let's see if there's any of those current buns going spare. Maybe a drop of tea.'

Not so many minutes later Reg Simpson came in and called the men to order. Standing by his side was a youngish-looking man in fire service uniform, rucksack on one shoulder, camera case hanging from the other.

'This here's Alan Prentiss,' Simpson said. 'He's one of the London Fire Brigade's official photographers and he's going to be joining us for a spell. Maybe, Alan, you could give us some idea of what that entails?'

'Course. Glad to. Broadly speaking, my task's documenting the Brigade's activities fully as I can. Be on hand at major incidents and get photographic evidence that can be used afterwards in any debriefing. Training, too.'

He had quite a strong accent, Jack thought.

Northern. Yorkshire or Lancashire, he wasn't sure.

'Before this little lot started,' Prentiss went on, 'the photographs could also be used to determine how a fire had started, sometimes, in the case of arson, leading to prosecution. Less likely these days, of course. Only too clear how most of our fires get started.'

'Bloody Hitler!' someone said.

'Bloody Goering!' said another. 'Fat bastard! Got in one of his own planes, bugger'd never get off the ground.'

Laughter all round.

'One thing more while you're all here,' Simpson said, raising a hand for silence. 'I've asked Alan if he'll take a group picture or two. For the archives. Something to remember this all by, when it's over.'

'Before you do that,' Charlie Frost sang out, 'better lock O'Connor here in the karzy, else his ugly mug'll bust the camera.'

O'Connor, an Irishman with an unfortunate squint, didn't take that lightly. 'Who'd you reckon you are then? Clark-ruddy-Gable?'

'Me?' Charlie Frost laughed. 'More Ronald Coleman.'

'In your dreams, you fat-faced . . .'

'Right, that's enough,' Simpson said sharply. 'Cut it out, the pair of you. I shall expect everyone back here bright and early tomorrow morning for this photograph. And not looking as if you've just crawled out of bed, if you please. Spick and span, that's what I want to see. Tunics ironed and buttons shining. And let's hope the bells don't go down before Alan here's clicked the shutter.'

Jack finished his bun, washed the last mouthful down with his tea, and was ready to be on his way. His dad exchanged a few remarks with a bunch of the others, shouldered his bag, and together he and Jack headed for the door.

They were halfway across the yard, when a voice called after them. Alan Prentiss, following briskly in their tracks.

'Ben, is it?' he said, holding out his hand. 'Ben Riley? And this is your boy, Jack?'

Jack, too, shook the photographer's hand.

'Your leading fireman was just telling me about Jack here being a Brigade messenger. One of the youngest, too, isn't that right, Jack?'

'I'm not sure.'

'Well, either way, the thing is this: so far there's been little documentation of what lads like yourself actually do. You boys on your yellow bicycles. So what I was wondering, how would it be if I found you some time when you're on duty, took a few pictures of what you do, where you go? Maybe get some sense of the kind of dangers this job gets you into.'

He paused to give Jack time to take it in.

'What d'you say?'

'I think . . . yes, I suppose that'd be okay.'

He glanced round at his father for confirmation.

'What do you think, Mr Riley? Ben? Would you have any objections?'

Ben shook his head. 'I don't think so, no.'

'Grand! That's agreed then. I'll catch up with you, Jack, as soon as I can.'

EIGHTEEN

The next five days were lost in a whirl of bicycle wheels and wailing sirens and all thoughts of Alan Prentiss and photography were forgotten. Five days in which the phone lines went down no less than nineteen times. Urgent messages had to be carried back to area headquarters from fire watchers on the high ground of Hampstead Heath and Primrose Hill; messages from ARP wardens battling with incendiaries; from auxiliary police officers patrolling City Road and Highbury Fields. Fire crews and equipment had to be shown the way from one incident to another, depending on need: a change in wind direction, say, causing a blaze to spread north-south as opposed to east-west.

When the bombing was at its most intense and crews

from outside London were called in for support, Jack found himself coming to the assistance of drivers who had taken too many wrong turnings along unfamiliar roads and become well and truly lost – roads, some of them, which were now little more than piles of immovable rubble – Jack guiding them through a maze of barely passable streets to their destination.

More than once, he jumped from his bike as soon as the fire was reached and led the way to the nearest hydrant, staying long enough to assist one of the men in attaching the hose before continuing his journey; at other times he helped to unravel the hose and remained with it until the water pressure had built up sufficiently for the firemen to advance towards the heart of the blaze.

Jack was in the station yard, mending yet another puncture – the second that day, and with all the glass on the roads, a miracle it wasn't more – when Alan Prentiss appeared, climbing out of one of the London taxis that were often used for towing the smaller trailer pumps when no other vehicles were available.

Walking briskly across the yard, the photographer held out his hand.

No one had been so keen on shaking his hand when he was still a schoolboy, Jack thought. Back then not many grown-ups had noticed him at all, other than to tell him to sit up straight and pay attention in class. All of which seemed so long ago: before the Blitz, before the war.

'You've not forgotten, Jack? This photo shoot of ours?'

'No. No, course not.'

'Good. I'll just have a quick word with your chief, make sure it's okay. Chain of command and all that.'

He winked and headed indoors.

A few minutes later, he was back. 'Looks like we're on. Phone lines are up and working, no major incidents reported and two regular despatch riders on duty, so, bar a sudden emergency, we're fine to get started.'

He began to free one of his cameras from its case.

'Soon as you've got that tyre back to rights, we can start with a few shots of you here in the yard.'

He began with Jack standing alongside his bike in uniform – then asked him to cycle round the yard a few times so as to catch him in motion, Jack manoeuvring between the various appliances waiting for action – a Pipe Tender and two Medium Trailer Pumps and, the station's pride and joy, a Turntable Ladder of the very latest design.

'Right. Now, how about you nipping outside, round the block to get up a bit of speed, and then whizzing back in here as if all the hounds of hell are at your backside? Jump off the bike and belt in to make your report fast as you can. Think you can do that?'

Jack thought he could.

Not once, as it turned out, but twice. Then a third time for luck.

By the time Prentiss was satisfied he had what he needed, Jack's face was bright with sweat.

'Good lad. We'll see what these look like and maybe sometime later I can get some shots of you in action during a raid for real. But for now, I reckon you've earned a break. There's a greasy spoon, I noticed, just past that picture palace, we could go there.'

The Forum was one of the cinemas Jack used to go to with his mum and dad on Friday evenings, regular as clockwork. When the war had started all the cinemas had been closed, for fear of being ready targets for bombs, but now, despite the Blitz, they were mostly open again.

The signs above the entrance were advertising *The Grapes of Wrath*, the posters reminding Jack yet again of the photographs of refugees he'd seen in *Picture Post* – a big old car crowded with what looked like a family and all their possessions, some people sitting on top, some clinging to the sides.

He wondered if Prentiss ever had his photos in magazines like *Picture Post*? If he had ever been abroad and photographed refugees?

'You been to see that?' Prentiss asked, pointing up at the cinema. '*Grapes of Wrath*?'

Jack shook his head.

'You should. Get your dad to take you on his night off. If he gets a night off, that is.'

'Even then, I don't think he will.'

'Why ever not? Don't tell me he doesn't go to the pictures?'

'No, he does. Least he used to. We all did. But what he really likes are Westerns. So that's mostly what we got to see.'

'Well, tell your dad the man who made this, he made a couple of great Westerns. *Stagecoach*, did you see that?'

'Yes. Yes, we did.'

'*Drums Along the Mohawk?*'

'I don't think so.'

'Anyway, try and get him to take you if he can. It's a sort of a Western, anyway, tell him.'

'Really?'

'Well, it is about a bunch of people headed West.'

They were level with the café Prentiss had called a greasy spoon, though it didn't seem too greasy to Jack. There were two off-duty firemen, tunics unbuttoned, sitting at the window table with large mugs of tea, enjoying a cigarette. A few older men sat at tables further inside, one reading the newspaper, one tucking into a plate of sausage and chips; another man unshaven, balding, a burn mark, livid, down one side of his face, was just sitting there, arms folded, staring off into space. Music was coming from a wireless set perched precariously on one end of the counter.

Prentiss ordered tea for himself, a bottle of Tizer for Jack; a fish paste sandwich and an apple turnover, both of which he cut in half to share.

'And now,' said the radio presenter, 'for a change of tempo, this is Billy Mason and his Orchestra playing "St Louis Blues".'

Jack bit into his sandwich, swallowed, and washed it down with a swig of Tizer.

'You like music, Jack?' Prentiss asked.

'I suppose so.'

'Noticed you tapping your feet as soon as this came on.'

For no good reason, Jack felt himself starting to blush. 'Sounds like the kind of thing my dad would listen to. Him and my mum.' He laughed. 'Sometimes they'd get up and dance. Right there in the living room. "May I have the pleasure," my dad says. And the next minute he's spinning my mum round and round.'

Prentiss was smiling at the image Jack presented. 'Sound like a happy couple.'

'They were.'

'Were?'

'My mum's had to go away. Some kind of war work, I don't know. Hardly ever see her nowadays.'

'You will, when this is all over.'

A lump caught in Jack's throat and he turned his head aside for fear he was going to cry.

Tactfully, Prentiss went back to the counter for a second cup of tea.

'How come,' Jack said, once Prentiss had returned. 'How come, earlier, you were using two different cameras?'

'Easy. This one, the little one – it's a Leica, by the way – is better if you want to catch something on the move. You on your bike, say. The other one, the one I was using earlier . . .'

'The one you were looking down into instead of holding up to your face?'

'Precisely. That's a Rollie. A Rollieflex Automat, to give it its proper title. That gives you a bigger picture, more detail, but it's not so good for anything moving at speed.'

'And they both work the same way?'

'More or less.'

'You press the . . . the shutter? Is that what it's called?'

'The shutter release, yes.'

'And then what?'

'Then you've got a photo.'

'But don't you have to take it to the chemist's first or something? That's what my dad does.'

Prentiss smiled. 'Well, that's one way.' He speared the

last piece of apple with his fork. 'What kind of camera does your dad have anyway?'

'Just some sort of square box thing. Nothing fancy like yours.'

'Box Brownie, probably.'

'I don't know what it's called.'

'They're fine for family snaps and the like. But if you're after something a bit more special you need something, well, a bit more sophisticated, I suppose. And just as important, you need to be able to develop and print it yourself.'

'Is that what you do?'

Prentiss nodded. 'When I can.'

He pushed away his plate and checked his watch. 'We'd better be getting back. But I tell you what, we'll make some time, air raids allowing. Next few days, maybe. I'll show you my dark room, where the magic all happens.'

'Magic?'

Prentiss laughed again. 'All right, not exactly magic. More a mix of chemicals, timing and good luck. But you'll be able to see for yourself. Okay?'

Jack nodded emphatically. Okay.

'Maybe after that, if you really are interested, you could have a go yourself. How'd that be?'

A broad grin spread across Jack's face. He thought it might be pretty good indeed.

NINETEEN

The flat where Alan Prentiss was staying was no more than a twenty-minute walk away from Jack's home, just the other side of the Holloway Road. Several of the houses had suffered bomb damage, some quite recent; one, Jack guessed, had been hit only the night before, the scent of burning still lingering on the air. A couple were bent low over the wreckage, searching for whatever they could rescue of their lives.

Number 34 was next to a small factory at the far end of the street; save for a few missing windows, both buildings seemed relatively unscathed.

When Jack rang the top bell as instructed, a window on the upper level opened and the photographer's head appeared.

'Here, Jack. Let yourself in and come on up.'

Two-handed, Jack caught the key.

The stairs were dusty and bare, the smell of cooking faint from behind closed doors.

Prentiss greeted him on the upper landing.

'Come on in, Jack. It's not much, but for now it's what passes for home.'

Chairs, a table, a small settee; a gramophone perched on a tea chest in the corner, a wireless set on the floor; black and white photographs pinned by clothes pegs to a washing line that had been hung diagonally across the room; piles of books and records leaning precariously against the walls.

There was a record playing, brassy and loud.

'You like jazz, Jack?'

'I don't know. I mean, I'm not sure. My dad's got this Fats Waller record he plays all the time. Is that jazz?'

'Fats Waller? You bet it is.'

'But this isn't . . .?'

'No. This is the wonderfully named J. C. Higginbotham and His Six Hicks.'

Jack laughed.

'But just hang on a minute and listen to this.'

Prentiss lifted the record that had been playing from the turntable and replaced it with another.

'Recognize it?' he asked after several moments.

'I'm not sure.'

'It's the same tune we were listening to in the café, but a different version. Louis Armstrong. You hear that trumpet? Nobody else plays like that. Nobody. I've got a friend who sends his records over from America specially.'

'All that way?'

'Worth it, Jack. All the way from the home of jazz.'

'My dad reckons sooner or later the Americans will come in on our side in the war. D'you think they will?'

'They did before. 1917. And yes, I think your dad's right. When they find out what Hitler's been up to in Europe especially, I think they will. I just hope they don't leave it too late . . .'

As if to emphasize what he was saying, as the record finished the sirens started up not so very far away, signalling the enemy's approach, the start of another raid.

'All right,' Prentiss said, 'the magic of the dark room, as promised. And this place being what it is, not exactly ideal, as you'll see I've had to improvise.'

In the small bathroom off the kitchen, three planks of wood had been placed across the bath, and, wedged into the corner, metal shelves had been bolted together like something from a Meccano set and were crowded with various pieces of equipment, the biggest of which Prentiss identified as an enlarger.

'Okay, there are basically two stages to all this.

Developing and then printing. And what we're going to do first is the developing. So if you pass me down the Leica from over there . . . Yes, that's it. What I'm going to do now is take the film out of the camera and slot it into one of these little spindle things . . . a reel, we usually call it . . . and that has to be done inside one of these bags . . .' Prentiss took what looked like an overlarge black tea cosy down from the shelf. '. . . so that it doesn't get exposed to the light. So, if you could switch off the overhead light and then switch on that little red light in the corner there . . .'

Lacking a window, the room lapsed into shadow, the red bulb casting a strange, faint glow. Prentiss' hands moved deftly inside the changing bag, working by touch.

'Good, that's done. Now if you'll hand me that thing that looks like a Thermos flask . . . Okay. I can pop the reel in there and we can move on.'

He pointed towards the middle shelf.

'Three bottles, you see, three different things we need. Developer first, stop bath next, fixer last. And before any of those, we should give this a quick rinse. If you'll edge back that middle plank, Jack, I can get to the tap.'

Prentiss filled the cylinder with water, shook it from side to side and then poured the water out. As Jack watched he carefully added the right amount of developer before passing the cylinder into Jack's hands.

'Right. I'm going to count up to thirty like this. One a-thousand, two a-thousand and so on. Once you've passed ten, leave out the "a". That'll give us thirty seconds. Okay? You count with me . . . twenty-seven thousand, twenty-eight thousand, twenty-nine thousand, thirty thousand. Now I'm going to shake this gently for another ten seconds. You got all that?'

'Yes, I think so.'

'Good, cause now it's your turn.'

Hesitantly, Jack took the cylinder from his hands.

'What you have to do is go through the exact same procedure ten times. That's all.'

'What if I get it wrong?'

'You won't.'

'But if I do?'

'The whole film's wasted. So start counting . . .'

Jack couldn't remember the last time he'd concentrated so hard.

As soon as he reached the last ten seconds, Prentiss took the reel back from him, emptied the developer away and, having asked Jack to pass the bottle of stop bath, poured some in and gave it a good shake for half a minute before that too was emptied away.

'Fixer, Jack.'

Once that was added, it was Jack's turn again to shake.

'Thirty seconds, Jack. Then we'll flush water through so all the chemicals are washed away. A couple of minutes, at least. After which, we take out the spindle and, carefully now, we remove the film and hang it up to dry. So.'

'But that's not . . .'

'Not a photograph. Not quite yet. Those are our negatives. What we have to do – what we can do, another day – is turn those negatives into positives. And, using a different set of negatives, I'll show you how. But right now, let's go back into the other room and have something to eat. I think it wasn't only *my* stomach rumbling I could hear during all that counting and shaking . . . Macaroni cheese, Jack, what do you say?'

While they were eating, Prentiss asked Jack about his family and talked a little about his own. His parents lived on a sheep farm in the West Riding of Yorkshire, and that's where he'd grown up, along with two elder sisters and a younger brother, who was in the Merchant Navy. One of his sisters was a nurse in a big hospital in Leeds, the other had three children of her own and was married to a vet, who she helped out on his rounds whenever she could.

'When did you first get interested in photography?' Jack asked.

'That'd be when I was round your age. This chap

came out to the farm one day, Peter, Peter Burchfield, taking pictures for a magazine. *Hare and Hound*, I think it was. He let me carry his stuff and that, tripod and so on. Took time to explain what he was doing.'

'Like you're doing with me.'

'Something along those lines. Told me if I ever wanted to earn a few bob, holidays and that, I could help him out. Be his assistant, if you like. My dad weren't too pleased. Meant time away from the farm and he needed all hands, lambing time especially. Still, one way or another, we managed and when I left school I went to work for Peter full-time. Nothing too exciting, mind. Weddings and the birthdays. Kiddies' portraits. But every once in a while he'd get one of these magazine assigments and we'd go all over. Up to Scotland, down to London.'

Prentiss laughed, remembering.

'That was how I first got interested in jazz. This American band was playing at the London Palladium. 1933, it would have been. Duke Ellington and His Famous Orchestra. Course, I didn't know him from Adam. Ellington. But Peter did. Said we had to go. Knew all manner of odd stuff, did Peter.'

He paused to fork up a last piece of macaroni.

'So there we were, front row of the circle. Variety, that's what it was. Music hall. Dancers, jugglers, comedians – Max Miller with a lot of smutty jokes, half the time you didn't know if it was okay to laugh or look away – and then, top of the bill, Ellington. The Duke. This big orchestra, right across the stage. Thirteen of them and all different shades of black, some black as the ace of spades. And the sound they made! Well, goes without saying, I'd never heard anything like it. Just twenty minutes or so they played and long enough to change my life, just about.

'I started buying as many jazz records as I could lay my hands on. And then I started photographing musicians as often as I could . . .'

'Jazz musicians?'

'Some. But really anyone with an instrument in their hands. Dance bands. Classical. Anything. Scraped a pretty good living out of it, too. Then, once it was obvious there was going to be another war, I talked my way into this job with the Fire Brigade.' He smiled. 'Hoses instead of saxophones.'

Prentiss reached across for Jack's empty plate and set it down on top of his own; carried them both to the sink.

'Let's leave these, I'll wash them all later. Time now for Making a Photograph, part two.'

In the bathroom, he set three trays, a bit like rectangular washing-up bowls, side by side.

'You remember before we used developer, stop bath and fixer?'

Jack nodded.

'We're going to use them again in the same order. And once they're ready, I'm going to take one of the negatives I've already processed, put it into the enlarger over here, take a sheet of photo paper and place that underneath. And now, more counting, thirty seconds from when I switch on. Okay, go!'

As soon as the time was up, Prentiss switched off the lamp on the enlarger and slid the paper into the developer; from there into the stop bath; then into the fixer, finally lifting out the finished print.

'Recognize that person?'

'It's amazing,' Jack said, seeing himself standing proudly alongside his bike in the fire station yard.

'I know. And no matter how many times I go through this, I never lose that moment of surprise when you see the image finally take shape. Come to life.'

He grinned.

'Like magic, eh, Jack? And now we'll just hang this up to dry and next time I see you I'll have this and a few more you can take home and show to mum and dad. Any girlfriends you might have.'

'I don't have any girlfriends.'

'No? Well, I'm sure one day you will. But right now . . .' Prentiss looked at his watch. '. . . you better be getting back home before it's too late. Busy day tomorrow, I don't doubt.'

* * *

Jack set off at a good pace, unable to stop thinking about the way Alan Prentiss had treated him when they were developing the photographs – almost as an equal. Even his dad didn't treat him like that. It felt special.

He quickened his step again and, as Louis Armstrong's version of 'St Louis Blues' echoed round his head, he started to whistle, a shrill sound that wavered into silence when he turned the corner and found himself facing the newly bombed-out house he'd passed earlier. There, in the gathering dark, the elderly couple who'd been searching for what remained of their possessions were boiling water on a small Primus stove to make themselves a forlorn cup of tea.

TWENTY

'See this, Jack?' His father passed the newspaper across the table, scattering toast crumbs in the process.

It was early morning, three days after Jack's visit to Alan Prentiss' dark room. As was often the case, while Jack was about to report for duty, his father had not long returned from a night of fire fighting down at the docks, one warehouse and a river boat saved, two storage depots and a landing jetty left in smouldering ruins. Smoke was clinging to his father's hair and deep in the lines of his face; his eyebrows were burned almost clear away.

Jack lifted the paper and folded it so that he could read the front page.

MORE BOMBS ON PALACE
The King and Queen Escape Unharmed

The King and Queen escaped injury yesterday when enemy 'planes deliberately bombed Buckingham Palace.

During a long daylight attack, which lasted from when the sirens first sounded at 9.45 a.m. until the All Clear at nearly 2.00 p.m., six bombs fell on Buckingham Palace, causing significant damage to the roadway at the front, the quadrangle at the back and to the royal chapel.

Both the King and Queen were in residence at the time and neither were injured.

This is the second occasion on which the Palace has been targeted. In the early hours of Tuesday morning, only two days previously, a 250-pound bomb fell close to the Belgian Suite, burying itself 10 feet deep and causing considerable structural damage. Once again, the royal couple, who had only recently returned from Windsor, were in residence at the Palace and unharmed.

'I'm glad we have been bombed,' the Queen is reported to have said. 'It makes me feel I can look the East End in the face.'

'What did she mean?' Jack asked. '"Look the East End in the face?"'

'Born the brunt of it, haven't they? Well, you know that as well as me. What your mum's folks have been going through. So bad that when they go down there, their royal majesties, Silvertown or Stepney or somewhere like that, telling people they're sure no matter what Jerry throws at them they'll put a brave face on it, well, it sticks in the craw. All very well for you to say – people think, some of them anyway – you're not the ones getting bombed night after night.'

'That's not their fault.'

'Maybe not. But not everyone sees it that way. Just last Monday, the King was booed by a crowd in Spitalfields. With that stammer of his, making himself heard's hard enough at the best of times.'

'Well, I think they're pretty brave,' Jack said. 'They don't have to stay in London, after all. They could be evacuated like I was.'

His father laughed. 'What? Be mucking out pigs on old man Granger's farm? That's something I'd like to see.'

'Dad, I'm serious.'

'Okay, okay, I'm sorry.'

'That's what the Dutch royal family did, after all. Left Holland and came here. It was in *Picture Post*.'

'I know. And then went on to Canada, some of them anyway. But that's different. Their country had been invaded. Overrun. They'd have been taken prisoner if they'd stayed. Or maybe worse.'

'What if we're invaded?'

Ben Riley shrugged. 'Who knows? Our royals'll be on a ship to Canada, too, I wouldn't be surprised. Either there or Australia.'

'And d'you think we will?'

'Be invaded?'

'Yes.'

Ben Riley blinked and sighed. 'I don't know, son. I really don't know. But we can't put up with this day in, day out, not forever, I know that. And not for so very much longer.' He pushed back his chair. 'Something's got to happen, change, but I don't know what.'

Slowly, he got to his feet, tiredness in every movement, every limb.

'I'm going to get me some kip. You should be on your way any time soon.' Reaching down, he gave Jack's shoulder a squeeze. 'Don't worry, son. It'll sort itself out. You'll see.'

Jack couldn't be sure, but when his father turned away there seemed to be tears in his eyes.

At first, Jack thought it was going to be a quiet day. The sirens had sounded early on, but proved to be a false alarm. Hopeful voices around the station suggested the Luftwaffe had decided to give London a miss. 'The submarine works down at Woolston,' reckoned one, 'that's what they'll be after.' Though no one seemed to know exactly where Woolston was. 'Birmingham way,' suggested somebody else. 'New Street station, that's been bombed before.' 'Merseyside,' was someone else's suggestion: 'the docks up there.'

Nobody knew for certain.

Jack tried to brush it all from his mind.

Having checked that the phone lines were all up and working and there had been no sightings of enemy planes, he borrowed a pack of cards and started to play one of the games of patience his mum had taught him when he was younger. He was just placing the red jack on to the black queen, when the sirens started up again, and this time it was for real.

Before long he heard the brittle chatter of ack-ack guns and the low drone of heavy aircraft drawing closer overhead.

Fifteen minutes or so after the first bombs fell, the phone lines went down.

'Jack, lad. Get yourself down to Clerkenwell with this. Division HQ. Sharpish, mind. See if there's anything urgent they need you for and if not, get yourself back here.'

For the bulk of the remaining day, Jack shuttled back and forth between Euston and Camden Town, Islington and Holloway, Primrose Hill and Finsbury Park. His legs ached and his lungs were sore from all of the effort he'd put out, the smoke he'd inhaled.

He was pedalling slowly back, shift over, muscles aching, when he turned south off Seven Sisters Road into a scene of almost utter devastation. A row of terraced houses had been largely reduced to formless rubble, a small and exhausted band of rescuers burrowing through the fallen bricks and mortar in search of survivors.

Futile as it looked, he remembered the small boy he had helped save when all hope seemed to have been lost. Remembered the story Lilith had told him about her sister, for whom hope alone had not been enough.

For the best part of an hour he laboured alongside the others – perhaps a dozen in all – until, dusk closing in, they were rewarded by the faint sound of knocking and, tunnelling faster, finally reached down to find three generations of a family – grandfather, mother and eighteen-month-old baby, the grandfather no longer conscious but alive – crouched together beneath a heavy door that had fallen in such a way as to form a roof above their heads and prevent them from being crushed.

Hands cut and grazed, fingernails cracked and torn, every muscle, every sinew sore, Jack just had energy enough to climb back on his bike and be on his way.

Never give up, he thought. That was what you had to learn. What all this taught you. If you did that, maybe his dad was right: things would sort themselves out for the best.

TWENTY-ONE

It did seem, for the next few days, as if his father might be on to something. For reasons that were less than clear – a change in the enemy's strategy, shifting patterns of the weather, a heavier than usual presence of RAF Spitfires patrolling the Channel – raids on the capital dwindled down into single figures. Not only that, the sun slipped out from behind the clouds, the temperatures climbed. Indian summer, Jack heard people call it, without ever really knowing why. At the Chester Road sub-station where his father was stationed, it was time for the vehicles and equipment to be brought up to scratch and then polished within an inch of their lives.

'I want to be able to see my ugly mush looking back at me from every panel, every piece of glass, every handle,' Reg Simpson told his men, and they did their best to make sure that he could.

Down in Kentish Town, Jack and one of the firemen took on Rose and Bobbie, the two despatch riders, in an impromptu game of soccer, which ended five-all when Rose, desperate to score a spectacular winning goal, skied the ball over the entrance and out into Highgate Road where it was promptly squashed flat by a passing goods lorry.

'You might as well get yourself off home,' the section leader told Jack just a little later. 'Make the most of a bit of peace while you can.'

By the time he arrived back at the house, his father was already there, boots off, braces dangling, smoking his pipe and reading Zane Grey's *Riders of The Purple Sage* for what had to be the umpteenth time.

'Dad, you must know every word of that book off by heart.'

'Near enough. Doesn't make it any less exciting. Here . . .' He passed it into Jack's hands. 'You should try it some time.'

Jack looked at the picture of a mounted cowboy on the yellow cover, twisting in the saddle to fire his pistol at the man pursuing him.

Turning the book over, he scanned the blurb.

The canyons and sage plains of Utah have a

dangerous beauty . . . Stories of a masked man and
a lone gunman looking for vengeance . . . and the
one brave woman whose courage stands out above
all else . . .

'No, thanks,' Jack said, handing the book back. 'Besides, I'm off out in a minute.'

'You've only just come in.'

'It's too nice to stay indoors.'

'Off to give Fred Campbell a hand, then?'

'Not exactly.'

Lilith was sitting outside in autumnal sunshine, sketching on a sheet of paper she'd attached to a makeshift easel. The object of her attentions: a scarlet geranium in a chipped terracotta pot that she'd balanced on a short stack of bricks. Seeing Jack, she waved a hasty greeting and continued working, pencilling in the crimped edges of the leaves that spread out in a cluster around the flower's stem.

Leaning his bike up against a remnant of wall, Jack went over and stood behind her.

'Don't, Jack. Please.'

'Don't what?'

'Stand there looking over my shoulder. I can't do this when somebody's watching.'

'But it's brilliant.'

'You think so?'

'I could never do anything like that in a million years.'

'I'm sure you could. But, Jack, just let me finish and then we can talk.'

'Okay.'

He went back to his bike and, bending low, checked the pressure in the tyres before testing the brakes and deciding the rear brake blocks were in need of adjustment. Then, Lilith still at work on her drawing, he reached towards the handlebars and, just for the fun of it, rang the bell. Not once, but twice; then twice again.

'Jack, stop. Stop, please.'

'What?'

'All that fidderling.'

Jack grinned. 'Fidderling?'

'I don't know, whatever the word is.'

'Fiddling. You mean, fiddling. Not fidd-er-ling.'

Lilith laughed. 'Now you have come to teach me English, I suppose?'

'No. I just came to make sure you were okay, that's all. Hadn't got yourself blown to pieces.'

'Well, that's nice of you. And as soon as I finish this . . . there . . . we shall have tea. Out here in the sunshine. While we can. You wait here, guard your fine yellow bicycle and my poor drawing. If you move some more of those bricks you could make yourself somewhere to sit.'

'And a little table?'

'Yes. Yes, Jack, some kind of table. That will be perfect.'

Inside ten minutes it was done. Maxie Freeman, the ARP warden, walking past on the opposite side of the street, touched the brim of his metal hat in salute and Lilith invited him over to join them.

'Another time, sweetheart. Sitting down to a cuppa with you and your young man, I'd be chuffed indeed. But right now, I've got places to go, things to do.'

And he continued, whistling, on his way.

'My young man, Jack,' Lilith said quietly. 'Is that what you are?'

Jack blushed.

'The warden seems to think so.'

'What does he know?' said Jack. 'Now why don't you just shut up and pass the sugar?'

It wasn't long before the sun had disappeared behind what remained of the buildings opposite, and it was too cold to remain outside.

Following Lilith down into the cellar, Jack noticed that she had added a solid-looking wooden crate that served both as cupboard and extra seat, and a narrow sheet of wooden panelling that she was using to display half a dozen or more of her sketches and drawings.

Flowers Birds. A distant view out across the heart of London that he recognized as being from the summit of the Heath. And, underneath, two small, carefully pencilled portraits of a woman with softly curling hair who looked like an older version of Lilith herself.

'When did you do all these?'

'I don't know. The last few days.'

'How come?'

'When I was younger – back at home – I used to be drawing all the time. Just little things, you know? Nothing special.'

'They look pretty special to me.'

'My mother, she was really good. We always said she could have been a professional artist if she'd wanted.'

'Is that her, there?' Jack asked, pointing.

'Yes. That's her. The way I remember her.'

'She's lovely.'

'Beautiful, I think.'

'She looks like you.'

Embarrassed at what he'd said, Jack looked away. The rare sound of a passing car troubled the silence between them.

'I . . . I ought to go. My dad'll start worrying.'

Leaning forward, Lilith kissed him on the cheek, the corner of her lips just brushing his, her hand resting briefly on his arm.

A second, perhaps two, that's all it was.

Jack swallowed and stepped back.

'I do have to go.'

Stumbling a little, he scrambled up the steps and out on to the darkened street. In the distance, the first sirens of the evening could be heard, sending out their warning; the temporary peace was over, the first searchlights searching, moth-like, across the blackening sky. With an involuntary shiver, Jack touched his fingers to his cheek before he swung his leg over the crossbar and rode thoughtfully home.

TWENTY-TWO

Jack scraped what was left of the margarine on to his last piece of toast, half an ear tuned to the morning news. 'Following a second successive high yield harvest on its prairies,' the newsreader said, 'the Canadian Minister for Agriculture yesterday assured his counterpart in His Majesty's government that sufficient surplus exists to provide for Britain's needs for the next three years should that become necessary.

'For the third night running,' he continued, 'enemy raids on London had been light, the majority of Luftwaffe attacks concentrating on the industrial heartland, with Birmingham and Coventry its principal targets.'

Jack reached across and switched off the radio.

There was half a cup of tea still in the pot, black as pitch and the milk all gone.

He heard the swing of the gate, footsteps approaching the front door and then a double knock. Alan Prentiss was standing there in his fire brigade uniform, a package in his hand, square and thin, brown paper tied up with string.

'Hoped I might just catch you before you went off on duty.'

'Just about leaving now.'

'It's okay, I won't keep you. But here . . . Give this a listen to when you've got a moment. You might just like it. Your dad, too, I daresay. Careful with it, though, it's easily breakable.'

And with that he was on his way.

Back inside, Jack placed the record on top of the gramophone lid, unopened. Time for that later. If he didn't get a move on, he'd be late.

He had barely arrived when the first siren sounded, enemy planes spotted moving northwards across the city in large numbers. Urgent messages were starting to come in from all over B Division; the first bombs dropping to the west of Primrose Hill; the clamour of bells as firemen raced across the yard and drivers revved their engines, anxious to be away. Before the first hour was over, more than half of the telephone lines had gone down and Jack was hurtled into action as the fires spread.

The rest of the day passed in a blur of almost constant action, voices raw from smoke as leading firemen shouted fresh orders against a background of blazing buildings and over the cries of people stranded on upper floors or trapped beneath fallen masonry.

For one brief moment, making his way at speed over the railway bridge at Chalk Farm, Jack thought he saw his father high up on the rooftop of a factory building, but before he could be certain, the man, whoever he was, had moved from sight and Jack was on his way into the heart of Camden Town.

By late afternoon when the all clear finally sounded, the light was already beginning to fade. Jack was close to exhaustion, his calf muscles tight as walnuts, his legs, when he tried to walk, threatening to give way beneath him. For fully fifteen minutes he sat on the ground, head in his hands, waiting until he felt strong enough to continue.

One look at him and the commanding officer told him to get himself home immediately and get some rest. There was no need for a second bidding.

It was all he could do to push himself those last few hundred yards up the slight slope towards home. Bike safely put away, Jack splashed water on his face, washing away the worst of the smoke and smuts, pulled off his uniform and fell into bed. Within minutes he was fast asleep.

When his father came to wake him, he was dreaming. Walking on a beach, a beach he didn't think he'd ever seen. Bare feet leaving prints across the sand. Somewhere he'd never been. The water a strange sort of bluey-green, frothing at the edges as it bubbled up and fell back with the tide. A couple walking ahead of him, a man and a woman in swimming costumes, holding hands. The woman breaking away and running down towards the water's edge. Turning her head towards him and calling. His mother, the sunlight catching the drops of water sparkling on her skin. *Come on, Jack. Come on.* When he tried to run the sand seemed to cling to his feet and pull him back. *Jack, come on!* The more he struggled the further he fell behind.

'Jack, let's be having you.' His father's hand on his shoulder, shaking him awake, the dream disappearing like sand through his fingers.

His father's face.

'Mum, is she here?'

He shook his head. 'Here? No, why? Whatever made you think that?'

'I heard her. I thought I heard her.'

'You must have been dreaming.'

Sitting up, Jack rubbed the sleep from the corners

of his eyes.

'Treat this morning,' his dad said, grinning. 'Bacon and eggs.'

'How come?'

'One of the blokes at the station. Flogging off rashers of bacon. Black market, I dare say, but what can you do?' He winked. 'Ask no questions, you'll hear no lies.'

By the time Jack was washed and dressed, the smell of frying bacon was filling the little kitchen. And there was the sound of music coming from the other room. Piano. A voice. Then the sound of a trumpet and the voice again. A man's voice, full of laughter.

'I don't know where it came from – not Christmas, so it didn't come down the chimney, but someone left it on top of the gramophone.'

'That was the photographer . . .'

'Prentiss?'

'Alan, yes. He brought it round. Said I might like it. You, too.'

'Well, he was right. Fats Waller and his Rhythm. Just up my street.'

The record came to an end, and his dad went quickly into the next room and lifted the needle clear. A quick turn of the handle and he set it to play again.

'Day off today, haven't you?' his dad said when he sat back down.

Jack nodded.

His dad grinned. 'All right for some. Still, maybe go up Parliament Hill, eh? Take the camera with you.'

'I'll see.'

He wasn't sure what he wanted to do. Maybe once his father had gone back on duty, he'd go back to bed. Catch up on lost sleep. See if he couldn't get back into his dream.

He didn't know it then, but Lilith had other ideas.

TWENTY-THREE

He wasn't sure if what he heard first was her voice or the tinny ringing of a bell. Whichever it was, it got him to the front door and there she was, astride the oddest looking bicycle Jack had ever seen.

'Jack! Jack!' she shouted eagerly, the moment she saw him. 'Look! Look. I built her all myself. Isn't she beautiful?'

Not a word I would have chosen, Jack thought.

From somewhere, Lilith had found a discarded frame, to which she had somehow attached two wheels of differing sizes and a pair of handlebars so ancient Jack thought they could have come out of the ark. Had Noah been a cyclist.

'It didn't seem fair,' Lilith said, 'if you were the

only one of us with a bike to ride. And now we can go on adventures together. A grand bicycle ride, eh, Jack, what do you think?'

Jack could not help smiling.

'And where will we go exactly? On this grand bicycle ride of yours?'

'A long way, Jack. Quite a long way, I think.'

'But where?'

'A secret, Jack. A secret for now. You will trust me, yes?'

'Maybe.'

'Oh, Jack . . .'

'And besides, never mind going a long way, if you can ride down to the end of this street and back without one of those wheels falling off I'll eat my hat.'

Lilith laughed. 'First of all, I don't believe you even own a hat. Aside from your helmet, that is. And I don't think you would ever be able to eat that. And secondly, I will make you just such a bet that the only thing to fall from this fine machine between here and the end of the street will be a small amount of rust.'

'You say.'

'Yes, I do. So, Jack, do we have a bet or no?'

'That depends.'

'On what?'

'On what we're betting, exactly?'

'If no harm comes to my bike between here and the

end of the street, you will agree to come with me, no questions asked.'

'All right, you've got a deal.'

Not much more than ten minutes later, Jack was following Lilith across the junction by the tube station and up on to York Way. Once they had worked their way through to the Caledonian Road and from there down towards the Old Street roundabout, Jack had a pretty shrewd idea of where they were heading.

The closer they came to the East End, the worse the devastation around them became: small factories and workshops demolished, houses that looked as if they had been hurled up into the air by a giant hand, whole streets flattened.

And now Jack was sure.

He remembered the tears on Lilith's face when she had told him what had happened to her family, her sister . . . *ever since then, I have felt guilty to be still alive.*

The house where Lilith had lived with her aunt and sister still had one wall standing, two storeys high. Patterned wallpaper, above and below, a single edge flapping in the wind. On the upper level, a shelf still stood, bracketed to the wall.

Everything else was dust and broken brick, splintered lath and plaster. You could still see where the salvage teams had thrown the rubble aside as they burrowed down to find survivors who had not been there.

For some moments Lilith stood, head bowed in prayer, Jack hanging back, keeping a respectful distance.

Then she lifted her head, turned smartly round, and took from the straw bag she'd attached to her handlebars a jam jar filled with water, the lid screwed carefully back on, and a small bunch of flowers, pink and yellow roses and a few small-headed chrysanthemums.

These she arranged neatly and placed in the shelter of the surviving wall.

'She would like those, Jack, my sister, the roses.'

'They're beautiful.'

'Thank you, Jack.'

With a quick squeeze of his hand, she stepped away.

'And now,' Jack said, 'I've got a surprise for you.'

At first Jack thought there was no one in. He knocked and knocked again, then lifted the letter box and peered inside. Nothing but grey stillness, silence. But then the sound of a voice, muffled, and footsteps, slow and shuffling, coming towards the front door.

'Jack!'

'Hello, Grandad.'

'Blimey, boy, never expected to see you today. Caught me napping, an' no mistake.'

Terry Bentham's hair was tangled and awry, the lines from whatever his head had been resting on – cushion or pillow – etched deeply into his cheek.

Carefully, he rubbed his eyes and blinked. 'And who's this then? Lady friend, I suppose?'

'No, Grandad, I . . .'

'Hello, pleased to meet you. I am Lilith, Jack's friend.'

She held out her hand.

'Well, Lilith, Terry Bentham, at your service. You're welcome, I'm sure.'

His hand was warm and rough around hers.

'Jack, you've got a chain for your bike, I reckon. Best lock 'em both up together, be on the safe side. Tea leaves by the dozen round 'ere and no mistake.'

'Tea leaves?' Lilith looked puzzled.

'Rhyming slang. Tea leaves, thieves.' Bentham glanced back over his shoulder. 'Inside here, you've got your apples and pears, see?'

'Stairs,' Lilith said, with a smile.

'Right. Apples and pears, stairs. Catch on quick, don't she? Got a bright one here, Jack, though what's she's doin' with you's another matter altogether. Shortage of fit blokes a'cos of the war, I reckon.'

Jack glared, starting to blush.

'Please, Mr Bentham, it is not fair to tease him.'

'No? Okay, then, p'raps you're right. Come on

inside, the pair of you. I'll just have a quick sluice, splash some water in me face, then get the kettle on.'

They sat slightly awkwardly side by side on the small settee, while Terry Bentham busied himself in the kitchen.

'Where's Nan?' Jack called.

'Over Chingford way. Gone to see her pals. Every month, like clockwork.'

He chuckled as he came back in with tea and biscuits on a metal tray.

'Take more'n ruddy Hitler to keep them girls from getting together. Known one another since they was nippers, you might say. Started kindergarten together, juniors the same. Left school on the same day, too. Not so long after your nan's fifteenth birthday.'

Setting the tray down on the small table, he pulled round one of the chairs and sat down.

'Clever she was, your nan. One of her teachers, he reckoned she should've stayed on longer. Took her School Certificate. But there was nine of 'em at home, six of 'em younger and four of 'em boys. They needed her to be out earning a wage.'

Carefully, he poured the tea.

'Me, the school couldn't wait to kick me out the door. Fourteen, I was, a scrawny little kid with bugger all sense and the arse hanging out me trousers.

Excuse my language. Got a job runnin' errands for a greengrocer's down on the high road, and after that the docks. Never missed a day's work till I retired. Or, tell the truth of it, they retired me.'

He stirred two sugars into his tea.

'How I managed to get hooked up with your nan, Jack lad, what she ever saw in me, Lord only knows.'

'I expect you charmed her,' Lilith said, smiling. 'That's what it was.'

The old man laughed. 'Sweetheart, I think you might've hit the nail right on the head.'

When Jack's nan arrived home not so much later the teapot was brought into service again, and Lilith, who, under questioning, had already told her story – her family's story – once that afternoon, was pressed into telling it again.

The bare facts: no tears.

Jack's grandparents listened in sadness and surprise. Admiration for Lilith's bravery and fortitude.

'I don't suppose you've heard anything from your mum?' his nan asked Jack as they were leaving.

Jack shook his head.

'That wretched place they've sent her to. I don't know what they're doing there, all this hush-hush business, but whatever it is, it better be important. Keeping them cooped up like prisoners of war.'

'We're all a bit like that,' his grandad said, 'one way

or another. Every damn one of us. And that's a fact.' He looked at his watch. 'And I don't want to be tellin' you two what to do, but don't you think maybe you ought to be heading back before all hell starts to break loose again?'

When they got back to his house, Jack thought, before she rode off, Lilith might take it into her head to kiss him again. Embarrassed that she might and not knowing how to respond if she did. But instead she simply smiled and touched his hand for a moment with hers, then swung her bike around, and, thanking him once again for coming with her, rode off down the road, Jack watching her until she was out of sight around the bend.

TWENTY-FOUR

It was two days later. A glowering sky promising rain and worse. Jack was on his way back from Division HQ, taking a short cut past one end of Chapel Street market, when a dark saloon car passed close by him and drew to an abrupt halt just ahead, blocking his path.

Jack's mind flashed back to the hijacked lorry, imagining someone jumping out at him, wielding an iron bar.

Veering right, he rode his bike up on to the crowded pavement, seeking a path between the shoppers coming out of the market and earning himself more than a few dirty looks and shouts of rebuke.

Ahead, a man stepped out from the back of the car and raised a hand for him to stop.

Detective Sergeant Reardon.

Jack braked and drew to a halt.

The detective was wearing a rumpled raincoat and a battered-looking trilby hat, the brim down.

'Jack, didn't mean to startle you. Just thought I'd like a word.'

'What about?'

'Why don't you get in the car? My driver'll keep an eye on the bike, make sure it don't get nicked.'

The interior smelt of mints and stale cigarettes. Reardon took off his hat and lobbed it on to the front seat, pushed a hand up through his hair. One of his eyes, Jack noticed for the first time, had a greenish tint in one corner, the other plain grey.

'Your dad okay?'

'He's fine, why?'

'No reason. Just, you know . . .'

Jack waited.

'You remember a few weeks back now, there was this big fire in the West End, back of John Lewis, Cavendish Square?'

'Yes, I remember.'

'You'd gone down there with a message, fresh orders I suppose?'

'For Blue Watch, yes. There were these people trapped up above some shops.'

'Blue Watch, that's your dad's unit?'

'Yes.'

'So he would have been there?'

'Yes, of course.'

'Those shops you mentioned, can you recall what they were?'

Jack thought back. 'There was this place selling wedding dresses, I remember that. One of them went up in flames right in front of me.'

'Anything else?'

'A jeweller's, I think. I'm not sure about the rest. The front of the shops were more or less destroyed. Most of the insides, too.'

'Which men from Blue Watch were tackling that part of the fire, can you remember that?'

'Not really, no.'

'Your dad?'

'Maybe. I don't know.'

'But it's possible?'

'Yes, I suppose so, but there's no way I could be sure. I got hit by some flying glass and I was out of it for a while. By the time I came round, everything had been brought more or less under control.'

'And there's nothing else you remember?'

'About the jeweller's?'

'Yes.'

'Someone said something about the safe still being

all in one piece despite everything. I can't think of anything else.'

'And, safe aside, d'you know what happened to the other contents of the shop?'

Jack shook his head. 'No, sorry. I've got no idea.'

Reardon seemed to be about to say something else, then changed his mind. Reaching across, he pushed down the handle on the car door.

'Okay, then, Jack. You'd best be getting along. Oh, and Jack, if you do happen to clap your eyes on that green Austin from the hijack, you'll be sure to let me know?'

One look at his father's face and it was obvious he was in a foul mood. That and the way he merely grunted when Jack asked him how his last forty-eight hours with Blue Watch had been. And if that weren't enough, the force with which he slammed the macaroni cheese down on the table simply underlined it all.

No sense, Jack knew, in asking what was wrong.

It would come out in its own good time.

Which was later on, the meal over, plates cleared and then cleaned; Jack doing the drying up while his dad tamped tobacco down into the pipe he sometimes, if rarely, smoked.

'That bloody Reardon!'

'What about him?'

'All but accusing me . . .'

'Of what?'

'It doesn't matter.'

'Dad . . .'

'I said, it doesn't matter.'

Jack sighed and lifted a plate from the draining board; his father struck a match and lowered it to the bowl of his pipe, cursing when it went out and when he went to strike another pressing so hard the match snapped in half. More cursing, Jack having to turn away to hide his smile. Finally, his father got the pipe going and Jack filled the kettle and set it on the stove, ready to make tea.

Apparently, half a dozen or so watches have showed up on the black market. Swiss. Expensive. Reardon reckons they're from that jeweller's at Cavendish Square. The fire, you remember . . .'

Jack nodded.

'Not just watches neither. A bracelet, sterling silver. Pearl necklace. Gold rings.'

'All from the same place?'

'So he reckons. Watches, certainly. Bracelet, too.'

'But he can't think you . . . You'd never do anything like that. Never.'

'That's not what Detective Sergeant bloody Reardon thinks. More or less come straight out with it, accused me to my face.'

'But he didn't?'

'Not outright, no.'

'Why would he think that, though, I don't understand?'

Ben Riley lifted the kettle from the stove, poured a little boiling water into the pot and swilled it round before emptying it out again into the sink and spooning in the tea. Making sure the water was still boiling he added it to the pot.

'It's not just me he's been questioning, it's everyone else on duty that evening, there at the Square. Whoever took the watches and that, he's convinced it had to be one of us.'

'That's not fair. Anyone could have taken them. Anyone.'

'Maybe so. But from where he's standing, you can see why he'd reckon most likely it was one of us.'

'And is that what you think too?'

His dad exhaled a slow breath and shook his head. 'Just a few days after we were at that raid on Cavendish Square, Charlie Frost took me to one side in the pub. Asked me if I wanted to buy a Swiss watch, going cheap.'

TWENTY-FIVE

A programme of light music was interrupted to relay the Prime Minister's speech. His first words were stark and unsparing, weighted with meaning.

> *Fourteen thousand civilians have been killed and twenty thousand seriously wounded, nearly four-fifths of them Londoners. But . . .*

And here, Churchill paused momentarily before continuing with greater resolution.

> *But none of the services upon which our great city depends – water, fuel, electricity, gas, sewerage – not one has broken down. On the contrary, although*

there must inevitably be local shortages, all the authorities concerned with these vital functions of a modern community feel that they are on top of their job.

Ben Riley reached over and switched off the radio. 'Listen to Winnie, you'd think we were winning the war instead of losing.'

'Is that what we're doing?' Jack asked.

'Losing?' His father sighed and scraped back his chair. 'I don't know. Who's to say? But if Churchill's saying fourteen thousand dead, you can bet it's a whole lot more.'

'You mean he'd lie?'

'If he thought it'd help, of course he would.'

'But why?'

'Never let the enemy know how much damage they're really doing. Besides that, put a brave front on it, bolster up morale. If you end up making it sound rosier than it really is, well . . .' He laughed. 'You know what they say, all's fair in love and war. Speaking of which . . .'

Jack read the twinkle in his father's eye. 'Dad, don't. Okay?'

'Don't what?'

'You know.'

'What?'

'I just don't want to talk about it.'

'I was only going to say . . .'

'Dad!'

'When are you going to ask her round . . .'

Jack was on his feet and heading for the door.

'You've taken her to see your grandparents, after all. I just thought you might like to invite her round one day for tea . . .'

But his last words fell on deaf ears. Jack was on his way outside. He thought he might have a slow puncture in his rear tyre and that needed dealing with before he set off. Whatever was going on between himself and Lilith, other than the fact they were good friends, he didn't want to play it out under his father's no doubt amused gaze.

He'd been on duty less than an hour when the first warning sirens sounded; it was not much longer before the first phone lines went down and he was sent into action with an urgent message from divisional HQ to central control. Despite the Prime Minister's bold assurance that all crucial services were continuing to function, undisturbed, the Fleet sewer had been breached by a parachute mine, with the result that one of the main tunnels into King's Cross railway station had been flooded.

Shortly after this, an enemy raid targeting the

railway depot close to Wembley Stadium resulted in a number of fires, not just around the depot, but amongst the tightly packed terraced streets that stretched south and west towards the Harrow Road. Miraculously, the stadium itself seemed to have escaped virtually unharmed.

Bombs continued to fall right across London, all but demolishing department stores in Bayswater, churches in the City, and a children's home in Finsbury. By nightfall Jack was exhausted, his muscles aching, every exposed part of his body blackened by smoke and soot. He was wearily making his way home, passing the front of Burghley Road school, when a car moved smoothly past him and stopped at the lights.

An Austin saloon with a curved back, bottle green. TLR 748

Not a 3, then, but an 8. Always assuming this was the same car.

The lights changed and Jack followed the car as it turned right along Fortess Road, down past the Working Men's Club and the church, slowing as it came level with the post office then turning left into a narrow stretch of cobbled road, little more than an alley, that led to some garages and a motor repair shop.

Jack continued on to the next set of lights, by the Assembly House pub. If he went left and left again that would bring him round to the garages from the other side. By the time he arrived, only moments later, the car had disappeared from sight.

Dismounting, Jack rested his bike up against the nearest wall and made his way forward, cautiously, on foot.

A light showed dimly from behind one of the garage doors.

Half a dozen careful steps closer and the light went out.

Jack held his breath.

The garage door opened and closed. A man emerged into the shadow, turning to secure the padlock before taking a step away then pausing to strike a match for his cigarette.

In the brief flare that illuminated the lower part of his face, Jack saw enough to recognize the same man who had masterminded the lorry hijack at King's Cross. The same features beneath the same hat.

Jack moved back and as he did his shoe struck something metallic that had been left on the ground and sent it skittering across the cobbles.

'Who's that?' the man shouted. 'Who's there?'

Jack turned fast, grabbing his bike and swinging it round as the man ran towards him, one foot seeking the pedal, the other pushing away. Within seconds, he was back on the main road, head down, leaving the man's angry shouts in his wake.

Instead of turning right towards home, Jack took the opposite direction, heading for the police station on Holmes Road.

The uniformed constable on duty at the desk didn't take his request to see Detective Sergeant Reardon particularly seriously – why didn't he come back in the morning and try then? It was only when Jack insisted that the PC phoned through to CID, and, after a brief conversation, grudgingly said someone would be down straight away to take him upstairs.

Reardon met him at the door. 'You're in luck, Jack. Just caught me about to call it a day. But come on in. What's all the fuss?'

Sitting across from the detective at his desk, Jack explained what he'd just seen.

'And you're sure it was Crella? You're certain?'

'Yes. At least, I think so.'

'It was dark, Jack, you said so yourself.'

'I know. But the car, that was the same, I swear.'

'The car from the hijack?'

'Yes.'

'All right. Let's see what we can do.'

He reached for the phone on his desk.

Within ten minutes there were police cars at each end of the alley, blocking any possible escape route, and officers were approaching the garage Jack had pinpointed from both directions.

The padlock was quickly snapped open with steel pincers, the doors pulled wide and torches shone inside.

Save for two spare tyres and a can of engine oil, the interior was empty.

Jack stared inside in disbelief.

'You're sure this is the one?' Reardon asked.

Jack was sure.

One of the police officers was bending over a patch of oil on the garage floor.

'This is still warm, guv. There was a motor here recent and no mistake.'

Reardon rested a hand on Jack's shoulder. 'Looks like you were right. Whoever was driving that car must think they've good reasons for keeping under the radar. And if it was Crella – and as I say it was dark and difficult to be certain – it could mean the rumours we've heard about him and the Kentish Town mob are likely to be true. Anyway, in your debt again, Jack. Keep this up and I'll be reminding you what I said about making a career in the Force.'

A quick handshake and the detective sergeant turned away. Minutes later Jack was back on his bike and heading for home. The adrenalin from the last hour or so had kept him alert, but now, with the air raid sirens sounding, all he wanted to do was crawl into the Anderson shelter and fall asleep.

TWENTY-SIX

While Jack slept, two bombs fell close to Burghley Road school, no more than half a mile away, missing the main buildings but leaving large craters in the playground, the blast taking out most of the windows, dislodging tiles. The bomber's intended target had most likely been the railway line that ran between the school and the edge of Parliament Hill Fields, which had been the object of several attacks before.

His father told him about it in the kitchen next morning. As was often the case, as Jack's day was just beginning his dad's was coming to an end. Breakfast for one, supper for the other. Toast with Marmite for the father, toast with marmalade for the son.

As for the school, Ben Riley surprised his son by

showing little sympathy. 'Shame they didn't bomb the place to pieces and have done with it. Long as there was nobody inside at the time.'

'I thought you went there?' Jack said. 'That's what you told me before.'

'I went there, all right. More's the pity.'

'Why? What was wrong with it?'

His father snorted. 'More a case of what was right.' He shook his head. 'Burghley Bug-Hole, that's what they used to call it, and that just about sums it up. Used to, those days anyway. Word is it's got a lot better since, but back then I hated the place. Never did me a scrap of good. Left when I was fifteen without learning a bloody thing. Except how to keep your thumb out the way when some cruel so-and-so's giving you the cane.'

'I had the cane once at school,' Jack said. 'It didn't hurt so much.'

'Once! Hardly worth mentioning. Once a week's more like it. Once a day, sometimes.'

'You're joking.'

'No, I'm not.'

'But what on earth for?'

Ben Riley laughed. 'Didn't seem to matter much what for. Being late of a morning. Not doing your homework. Talking out of turn. Answering back.' He laughed again, remembering. 'We played this trick on the Geography teacher once, me and one of the other lads. There was this blackboard and easel in his classroom, the blackboard resting, you know, on pegs. Before he came in at the start of the lesson, we rigged it so that the pegs, instead of being pushed right in, were only just about in place. First time he went to chalk something on the board it came crashing down on his toes.'

'He could have been really hurt.'

'I know.' Hurt or not, Ben Riley was smiling at the thought. 'Jumped up and down like a jack-in-the-box, he did. Swore like blue blazes. Said if whoever had done it didn't own up, he'd keep the whole class in for an hour after school.'

'So did you?'

'What?'

'Own up.'

'Not straight, away, no. But in the end we did. Had to. Wouldn't have been fair to the rest of the class, else. Couldn't let your mates suffer for something you'd done.'

'What happened?'

'Oh, we were trooped off to the headmaster. Left to stand outside his office wondering what was going to happen. If we'd be sent home, even expelled.'

'But you weren't?'

'No. Six of the best on each hand. A final warning.

And a letter from the head to our parents.'

'What did they say?'

Ben Riley grinned. 'Never saw it, did they? Got lost somehow on the way home.'

'And the school never checked?'

'More important things to do.'

'I'm glad my school wasn't like that.'

'You used to complain about it enough.'

'It wasn't so bad really. We used to have a good laugh sometimes. And some of the teachers were okay. Made it interesting. History, especially. English, too, sometimes. When you could write your own stories and that.'

Jack bit into his last piece of toast.

'D'you think I'll go back to school again? When this is all over?'

'Hard to say. Would you like to?'

'I'm not sure. But, yes, I think so. Not so much school. College, maybe. Somewhere I could learn something useful. Like photography.'

'Well, we'll see.' Ben Riley lifted the teapot, weighing it in his hand. 'Drop more if you want?'

'No, you have it. I'm okay.'

Jack still hadn't told his dad about what had happened the night before involving Vincent Crella's car and the police. He wasn't sure if he should. He could see his father being angry with him for sticking his neck out when it wasn't really necessary. Risks enough in being a messenger, he could imagine him saying, never mind getting involved in something that doesn't really concern you. Let the police get on with their job and you get on with yours.

Jack hesitated, the first words caught on the back of his tongue.

His father swilled down the last mouthful of tea and got to his feet. 'If you've got time to wash this lot up before you leave, I'll try and get a few hours' sleep.'

'Okay.'

'Just make sure you take care, right? Don't go taking any unnecessary risks.'

'I won't.'

His father was at the door.

'Dad . . .'

'Yes?'

'You know what you were saying the other day, about Charlie Frost and that watch?'

'What about it?'

'You don't think he really stole it, do you?'

'I don't know, son. I just don't know.'

'But if you thought he did, would you tell the police? I know you didn't then, but would you now? Now you've had time to think?'

'I don't know that either.'

His father left Jack to the washing up and his own

thoughts. Telling on a friend, even when you thought he was in the wrong, was that the right thing to do? He just didn't know. And if his father didn't, how could be expected to?

He wished there was someone he could ask, scmeone he could trust. Maybe, he thought, taking the tea towel from where it hung close by the sink, he'd ask Lilith, next time he saw her. That'd be the thing to do.

TWENTY-SEVEN

It was three days before Jack was to get the chance to talk to Lilith about anything at all. German bombers continued to cross the Channel with Messerschmitt fighter planes in support and, despite Spitfire squadrons going up to intercept them, large numbers succeeded in getting through. Bombs fell on Leicester Square and Chancery Lane in Central London and, once again, on the docks at Chatham and Rotherhithe. Further afield, there were raids on Birmingham and Coventry in the Midlands and Portsmouth on the South Coast.

The morning of the third day was shrouded in fog, which persisted through to the afternoon, hanging over the capital like a shroud. Visibility was similarly poor on the English side of the Channel, down along the coast from Dover and Folkestone as far west as Chichester and Southampton. Jack was released from duty early, still a good hour or so shy of evening.

After calling in on Fred Campbell to make sure he was all right – a bomb had fallen at the end of the street where he lived the night before – Jack made his way to Lilith's cellar retreat, meeting her, by chance, as she was making her way to the surface.

'Jack,' she said. 'Here you are and I thought you'd forgotten all about me.'

'That's daft.'

'Is it?'

'I've got a job to do, remember? I can't be coming round here every five minutes of the day to see if . . .'

'Jack, Jack . . .' Lilith was close to laughing now. 'I'm only teasing, can't you tell?'

'No, I can't. And if you are, it's not very funny.'

'Then I'm sorry. But, Jack, don't sulk, okay?'

'Who's sulking?'

Lilith did laugh then, shaking her head in amusement. 'Jack, I am sorry, really. You have found the time to come and see me and I should have been more – what is the word? Gracious? That's it. I should have been more gracious.'

'It's okay,' he said grudgingly.

'No, Jack, really, I'm sorry. But look, I was just going for a walk. Why don't you come with me? I've spent too much time today in that wretched cellar.'

'All right,' he said uncertainly. 'But where to?'

'Up across Parliament Hill and on to the Heath. That's what I was going to do.'

'On your own?'

'Why not? It will be safe enough tonight. There will be no more German planes, I think. What do you think, Jack?'

'I think you're probably right.'

Fifty yards or so along, Lilith slipped her arm through his, and despite his misgivings, Jack's face broke into a smile.

There was a bench near the summit and they sat there, looking down over London, not speaking. Shoulders just touching. Breath merging in the evening air.

Through the gathering gloom it was possible to see the heavier shapes of buildings far down amid the surrounding dark. Above, the sky yielded up no stars and as yet no moon. As he turned to speak, Jack's hand brushed against Lilith's arm, rested there for a moment, then moved away.

'Just suppose,' he said, 'you knew something about a friend, something they'd done that you knew was wrong, against the law even, what would you do?'

Lilith thought. 'It depends, Jack. What sort of thing?'

'Does that matter?'

'Of course. There are all kinds of wrong, some more serious than others. And if it is something truly serious, truly bad, then, of course, you should do something.'

'But what?'

'If it was me, and if it was a close friend, I would say something to them myself. Ask them about what they were doing. Ask them why.'

'And if they didn't listen?'

'Then I don't know. But why, Jack? Why do you ask?'

Jack told her about his father's suspicions about Charlie Frost. Alongside him, he could almost feel Lilith thinking it through.

'This Charlie,' she said eventually. 'He and your father, they are good friends, yes?'

'Yes.'

'Then I would ask him right out if the watch he had spoken of was stolen. If he said yes, tell him I thought it was wrong. But really, Jack, this watch, it is only a watch. I do not think it is so important.'

Jack still wasn't sure. He tried to picture himself in his father's shoes, what he might say then, what he might do.

'Let me tell you something, Jack,' Lilith said. 'A story. When we were still in Germany, in hiding much of the time like so many others, so many Jews, there was this family that my parents knew. They had arranged to leave the country – father, mother, grandmother and three little girls – a family just like my own – a barge was going to take them so far and then they would be guided across the country to the border.

'We said goodbye to them the night before and wished them luck. Promised that we would join them as soon as we could. They never arrived. We learned later that no sooner had they left the barge and started to make their way across the fields than they were surrounded by the Gestapo. The father was shot, trying to escape. The rest of the family were sent to the camps, I don't know which one. It was only after we'd arrived safely in England ourselves we discovered that one of their closest friends had betrayed them in order to save his own family.'

'That's awful.'

'I know.'

'How could anyone do something like that? I don't understand.'

'But it is life, Jack. Life now especially. When people are desperate, they will do many things. That is not to excuse. Not to say they are right. But when they are forced with their backs up against the wall and they can see no other way . . . I think we can begin to understand.'

'Even betraying their friends to the enemy?'

'To understand, Jack, is not the same as to forgive.

No, I think not. What that man did was terrible, awful as you say, and it will stay with him for the rest of his life. But compared to that, what is taking a watch, if that is what your father's friend has done? In times like these, we do what we can to survive.'

Is that why Charlie Frost had picked up that watch, Jack thought – if that was what he had done – and tried to sell it for a few pounds? Because he needed to survive? And how was that different from raiding a jeweller's in broad daylight or hijacking a lorry load of cigarettes?

Did it mean the more you stole the worse it was? Or were they all as bad as one another? He didn't know.

As if sensing his discomfort, Lilith touched his arm. 'Let's walk, Jack, shall we? Before it gets too dark to see.'

They had not gone more than a few hundred yards, the first clump of trees just coming into view, when they heard the high-pitched whine of aeroplane engines overhead.

Looking up, they saw a German plane – a Messerschmitt, Jack thought, from the body types he had learned – with a Spitfire in close pursuit.

The Messerschmitt seemed to be struggling to gain altitude, rising only a little as the Spitfire circled high above it then came soaring down, machine guns firing from both wings.

The Messerschmitt shuddered, body convulsing, nose to tail, before becoming engulfed in flame and dipping sharply, diving headlong towards the ground.

Lilith grasped Jack's hand and, just when it seemed too late, they saw the pilot eject from the blazing cockpit, the moon slipping from behind the clouds long enough to pick out the white of his parachute as it drifted across the night sky.

Then there was the wrenching sound of metal and a billowing cloud of black smoke rising to meet the gathering darkness.

TWENTY-EIGHT

The Messerschmitt crashed into trees near the northern edge of the Heath, both wings splintering free, the fuselage ploughing deep into a crater of its own making. By the time Jack cycled out there early the following morning, the Fire Brigade had rendered the site safe and a cordon of Air Raid Wardens and volunteers from the local Home Guard unit was keeping would-be souvenir hunters at bay.

Of the pilot, there was no sign.

Jack recognized one of the wardens as Maxie Freeman.

'No idea, Jack,' Freeman said, in answer to his question about the whereabouts of the German pilot. 'Parachute could have drifted off a good half mile from here, maybe more. There's police out looking for him, Territorial Army, too. If he's alive and somewhere in hiding, sooner or later they'll find him. Maybe later. Down Purley way, this Luftwaffe pilot was on the run for twenty-eight days before they brung him in. Been living off scraps from people's dustbins. Milk off the doorstep. This Jerry here, could be the same. Mind you . . .' He poked Jack with a finger, emphasizing every word. 'If I were a betting man, my money'd be on them finding him somewhere in the middle of the Heath, hanging from the branches of one of them trees.'

Jack hoped, if that were the case, he wasn't the one who came across him, face to face.

By the time Jack finished duty that day, the pilot had still not been found and rumours abounded. He had cracked his skull on landing and his dead body was stretched out in the undergrowth somewhere, exposed parts – face and fingers – being steadily eaten by foxes. He had, akin to Maxie Freeman's version, strangled to death when his parachute became entangled in the branches and the cords of the harness tightened around his neck. Or he had landed safely and now, armed with a bayonet-like knife and a pistol, was determined to survive for as long as he could and woe betide anyone who got in his way.

Both despatch riders had been talking animatedly

about the prospect of the German being still on the loose. Rose was planning to lock all of her doors and windows the moment she got in, and keep a rolling pin beside the bed just in case. After arming herself with a heavy-duty spade, Bobbie intended to check the various outhouses at the backs of her own and her neighbours' gardens, in case that's where he was hiding.

'What about you, Jack?' they asked, more or less in unison.

Jack didn't know.

His father was in the middle of a forty-eight hour shift and wouldn't be home. There was a tin of pilchards in the cupboard and, in the larder, some cold cooked potatoes and carrots that had come originally from Fred Campbell's allotment and were left over from the night before.

Jack switched on the wireless and set the frying pan on the stove.

The main item on the news was about RAF raids on German bases on the north coast of France. In England, tin helmets were going to be issued to postmen as part of a plan to reduce delays in delivery. The previous night's fog had caused a rise in the number of injuries to pedestrians on the roads in the capital. There was nothing about a German fighter plane being shot down over Hampstead Heath, nor a pilot on the run.

Following the news, said the announcer, there will be a selection of popular tunes played by Sandy MacPherson at the BBC Theatre Organ.

Jack turned the volume down.

He wasn't sure whether to put the pilchards on the same plate as the reheated carrots and spuds or to keep them separate and eat them straight out of the tin.

Having decided on the latter, he unfolded that morning's paper and sat down at the kitchen table with his supper. He'd just finished reading about the Spurs game against Arsenal, which had to be abandoned after forty-seven minutes due to an air raid, the Gunners three to two up, when he heard the first noise from the back of the house.

The wind, Jack thought, buffeting up against the rear door. He'd had to battle against quite a strong headwind coming home and, in all likelihood, by now it would be stronger still.

He turned the pages of the newspaper. Several hundred pounds' worth of black market goods had been recovered from a warehouse in south-east London; three arrests had been made and more were expected. A seventy-nine-year-old woman had been seriously injured in a road traffic accident in Peckham. There were weather warnings for the north of the country, with the promise of persistent heavy rain and gale force winds.

The back door rattled again.

Jack reached out and turned the volume on the wireless back up again.

'We'll Gather Lilacs in the Spring Again.'

The same tune that, in Jack's mind, seemed always to have been playing on Sunday lunchtimes, since back before the war had started. Just when his dad was carving the joint and his mum was draining the cabbage.

A man and woman singing about – what was it? – walking together down an English lane.

A horrible racket, Jack thought. He'd rather hear two cats squalling. He'd moaned about them more than once, not just their voices, which he truly hated, but the fact that they didn't even seem able to sing together, her voice never quite keeping up with his.

'That's how it's meant to be,' his mother had tried, patiently, to explain. 'It's called singing in harmony.'

That wasn't what Jack would have called it, but, wisely, he kept that to himself. Pinioning the last pieces of carrot on the tines of his fork, he ate them quickly, pushed back his chair and carried his plate across to the sink.

This time the sound was less of a knock, more of a thump.

Jack set down the plate; switched off the wireless and listened.

The kitchen door was ajar; beyond that there was just the small walk-in pantry and then the door to the garden.

He listened again.

Heard the faint brush of his own breathing and nothing else.

Lifting a torch from the shelf, he eased the kitchen door back wide. The air in the pantry was cold and slightly damp. The door to the outside two more paces away.

Jack strained his ears to hear. But there was nothing; it had all been his imagination. There was nobody there. He was just turning back when he heard something that stopped him in his tracks: the faint, but unmistakable sound of a human voice moaning in pain.

Quickly, Jack slid back the bolt, turned the handle and stepped outside. The figure of a man lay stretched out at his feet and it took only the briefest flick of the torch for Jack to see that it was the pilot from the crashed German plane.

TWENTY-NINE

Jack knelt alongside the pilot and felt for a pulse. At first he could feel nothing, but then there it was, almost imperceptible, the faintest of movements against his fingers.

Leaning back, he focussed his torch on the airman's face and was shocked by how young he looked. Not so very much older than Jack himself. Eighteen, he thought. Nineteen. Twenty at most.

Not frightening in the least.

There was a deep cut, partly scabbed over, to the right side of his face, beginning at the jaw and reaching up into his hairline, just behind the ear. More recent cuts and scratches to the rest of his face, as if he had been running – or crawling – through thick undergrowth.

The front of the blue-grey jacket he was wearing over his pilot's beige jumpsuit was darkly stained with blood, the jacket itself badly torn. Sewn to the left sleeve and still intact, was a patch showing his Luftwaffe insignia of two pairs of silver wings on a red background.

Shining the torch down along the pilot's body, Jack caught his breath. Where the right leg of the flying suit was badly torn and shredded across, a jagged edge of broken bone was poking through.

Jack shuddered as bile rose in his throat.

How the German had managed to get so far in that condition, a good mile or more from the section of the Heath where his plane had landed, Jack had no idea, unless the wind and the air currents had caused his parachute to drift in a more southerly direction than had first been thought.

Somehow though, Jack marvelled, he had kept himself alive for two days and two nights, evading capture, before finally collapsing where he was now, worn out, exhausted, presumably half-starving.

'Okay,' Jack said, speaking aloud though there were no signs the pilot could hear him. 'Let's get you inside.'

Moving round behind him, Jack bent low, reached under the man's arms and started to haul him towards the doorway.

At the first sharp tug, the German's head jerked backwards.

At the second, he screamed.

Carefully as he could, Jack lowered him back down.

Open, the German's eyes were blue, pale blue, and, seeing Jack's face, shot through with fear and pain.

'It's all right,' Jack said. 'I'm not going to hurt you.'

The German blinked and closed his eyes, head rolling to one side. Jack hurried indoors and fetched a glass of water, lifted the man's head and put the glass to his lips. After a few moments, he opened his mouth and drank deeply and too quickly, half-choking as he coughed most of the water back up again. Patiently, Jack tried again and this time the German was able to sip the water slowly and keep it down. With Jack's help, he shuffled backwards till the lower half of his back was resting against the wall.

'Jack,' Jack said emphatically, pointing a finger towards the centre of his own chest.

'Dieter,' came the reply, almost too quiet for Jack to hear.

He repeated it as best he could and the German nodded and managed what came close to a smile of understanding.

'All right, Dieter,' Jack said. 'Now with your help, and as painlessly as possible, we're going to get you safely inside.'

Jack just about managed to drag the barely conscious

pilot along the short hallway and into the front room, and there, level with the settee, was where he left him. For now.

Locking both the back and front doors just in case, Jack jumped on his bike. With any luck Maxie Freeman would be at the local ARP post and, if not, one of the other wardens would know where to find him. As it happened, Freeman was just setting out on his rounds when Jack arrived. He listened carefully, mind working – what to do, who to inform.

'Okay, Jack. You've done well, son. Brilliantly. Now get yourself back home sharpish. From what you've said, it doesn't seem as if our visitor's going to be taking off again on his own. Bit of a miracle he got as far as he did. So off you go. I'll get things organized here. Shouldn't be long, you'll have all the help you need.'

Needing no second bidding, Jack was on his way.

The pilot had scarcely moved.

When Jack spoke, called his name, 'Dieter, Dieter' over again, there was only the slightest of reactions, nothing more.

Within minutes, there was a knock, official sounding, at the front door: Maxie Freeman, along with two other Civil Defence workers, and two members of the Home Guard. They were joined, minutes later, by a doctor from the Hampstead General and North West London Hospital.

After giving the pilot an injection for the pain, he was carried upstairs and laid out on the bed where his uniform was partially cut away so that the doctor could examine him closely.

His shinbone was broken in two places, his right shoulder dislocated, and he had suffered severe lacerations and bruising to most parts of his body. Less than thirty minutes later, the doctor having done what he could to dress the German's wounds, an ambulance arrived to take him to the hospital under guard.

'What will happen to him?' Jack asked.

'They'll treat him,' Maxie Freeman said. 'Reset that shoulder, operate best they can on the leg. Soon as he's properly conscious, RAF Intelligence'll interrogate him . . .'

'And after that?'

'After that it'll be off to a Prisoner of War Camp out in the country somewhere. Made to do farm work, most likely. Though it'll be a while before that poor beggar'll be setting his foot on a spade or humping hay around on that shoulder.'

Freeman shook his head.

'Not much more'n a lad, really. Brave, too.' With his fist, he planted a mock blow on Jack's arm. 'Not the only one, eh, Jack? Handled yourself well there. Some would've panicked, but not you. Your old man'll be proud when he hears, I'll bet.'

THIRTY

Jack's picture was in the local paper, one of the photographs Alan Prentiss had taken showing him in his messenger's uniform. The Divisional Officer paid a special visit and insisted on shaking his hand. Rose and Bobbie rode their despatch bikes around him in the station yard while singing 'For He's a Jolly Good Fellow'. Bobbie went so far as to aim a congratulatory kiss on his cheek, but Jack ducked away at the last moment and she missed.

And there was a telegram from his mum.

MY HERO! CONGRATULATIONS. LET'S HAVE A CELEBRATORY PARTY THIS WEEKEND. LOVE MUM xxx

'Does that mean she's coming home?' Jack asked.

'What it sounds like,' his dad said.

Jack grinned at the prospect. With all the secret work she was doing – whatever that was – he hadn't seen his mum in ages. He could hardly wait for Sunday – even if it did mean listening to that stupid lilac song all over again.

The table was in the middle of the room, chairs set round. Best plates, best cups and saucers; from somewhere, cutlery Jack had scarcely seen before – cake forks, is that what those things were? Linen napkins, freshly ironed and then rolled inside silver rings. Sandwiches cut into triangles. Fairy cakes with dabs of coloured icing on top. And on a raised glass plate at the centre, a large slab of Battenburg cake, its alternating pink and yellow squares encased in marzipan.

As well as his mum and dad, Jack's grandparents, Doris and Terry, had caught the bus – two buses, actually – over from Whitechapel, and Fred Campbell had made the short walk along from Huddleston Road. And there, sitting opposite Jack, at the far side of the table, a blue bow in the side of her hair, was Lilith.

His mum had insisted.

'It's so nice,' she said, once they'd all settled and the first cups of tea had been poured, 'to know that Jack has made a friend.'

If she'd said girlfriend, Jack thought he would have jumped up and left the room. As it was, he blushed deeply and pretended to find something of great interest around the edges of his plate.

'Yes,' Lilith replied with a smile. 'It is nice for me, too.'

'Jack,' his mum said. 'Why don't you pass round the sandwiches?'

Still blushing, he did as he was asked and, with a little time, his embarrassment passed.

Lilith herself didn't seem in the least uncomfortable. She answered questions about her family and where she had come from, what had happened to them since arriving in England, without becoming teary or emotional. Only at the mention of her sister did her voice start to break, but she recovered herself quickly.

'We left some flowers there, didn't we, Jack? In the place where she died.'

'Yes,' Jack said, and felt strangely proud.

'Well,' Fred Campbell said, 'all I can say, young lady, is you're very brave.'

For a moment, Lilith bowed her head a little. 'We are all brave, I think, now,' she said. 'Even that pilot who crashed his plane. He was brave, too.'

'Funny sort of bravery,' Fred Campbell said, 'him and his lot, dropping bombs on innocent citizens.'

'I dare say,' Jack's grandad said, 'our boys are doing

much the same. War, it brings out the worst and best in all of us.'

That thought clouded the rest of the afternoon.

Jack's grandparents were the first to leave, wanting to get back before it became truly dark, and Fred Campbell left soon after. Jack's mum wrapped up what was left of the cake and gave it to Lilith to take with her.

'I hope it isn't too long,' she said, 'before I get to see you again.'

'Thank you,' Lilith said. 'You are very kind.'

'Well, Jack,' his father said, 'in that case I reckon you'd best walk your friend home, don't you?'

It's all right, Mr Riley,' Lilith said. 'There's no need. I shall be fine.'

'Nonsense. Bit of exercise. Just what he needs after stuffing himself with all that food.'

'All right, all right, I'm going,' Jack said testily, bending down to retie the lace on his shoe.

'Lilith,' Jack's mother said suddenly, 'just one thing before you go.'

Lilith looked at her expectantly.

'You could always come here, you know. To stay, I mean. Instead of camping out in someone's cellar. We have the room and we could make up a bed for you easily.'

'Oh, thank you, Mrs Riley,' Lilith said, 'you're very

kind. But I am used to my own little home. I feel safe there, way under the ground.'

'If you're sure?'

'I think so, yes.'

'Well, if you change your mind . . .'

Lilith smiled. 'Of course. And thank you again.'

They walked most of the way without talking, the light gradually deepening from pale yellow to a darker orange, closing them in. As they turned the corner of Lilith's road, her hand touched his, fingers slipping easily between his own.

'Your family . . .' she started to say.

After a moment Jack realized there were tears rolling, soundlessly, down Lilith's face.

'What is it? What's wrong?'

'Your family, they're so nice. And . . . and . . .'

He stood there, helplessly, watching her cry.

'I'm sorry,' Lilith said, wiping her face with her sleeve. 'It was a lovely afternoon, a lovely party, and now I've spoiled everything.'

Jack squeezed her hand. 'You haven't spoiled anything at all.'

'Are you sure?'

'Sure.'

'Good.' Lilith sniffed loudly and forced out a smile. The door above the cellar opening was secure and

Jack helped to move away the bricks that were holding it in place, then, between them, they slid it aside.

'I'd best be getting back,' Jack said. 'My mum, she's leaving again later.'

'Of course,' Lilith said. 'You must.'

For several moments, neither of them moved.

'Your mother, Jack, remember . . .'

'Yes.'

He wanted to kiss her but didn't know quite how, how to make that move, the space between them greater than a mere arm's length, impassable.

'Goodnight, Jack. Thank you for a lovely time.'

'Night.'

When he looked back from the far end of the street the darkness seemed to have swallowed her up.

THIRTY-ONE

The next day the weather cleared – no fog, little cloud, no rain – and the Luftwaffe were back with a vengeance. Jack's mum had already returned to her hush-hush job; his dad, along with the rest of Blue Watch, had begun another forty-eight hours on duty; and Jack, his small-scale heroics forgotten, yesterday's news, was busy ferrying messages from divisional HQ to units deployed all across their region and beyond, guiding everything from turntable ladders and trailer pumps to mobile canteen vans, away to unfamiliar destinations.

Through the daylight hours, a combination of RAF Spitfires and anti-aircraft guns had some success in keeping the German bombers from wreaking too much havoc on the centre of the city, but come evening more and more planes were breaking through the defensive cordon and finding a way to their target.

Altogether, forty-seven major incidents were reported and responded to across London, seventeen of those in B District's North Division where Jack was based. Euston station was targeted time and again, the main lines and the central platforms escaping with little serious damage, but two high explosive bombs leaving a huge crater in Seymour Street, close alongside.

The following twenty-four hours were worse: the number of incidents almost doubled. On Blackfriars Road, no less than five trams, busy with passengers, were hit during the evening rush hour, one bomb making a direct hit on the tram at the centre, crushing it completely and badly damaging the trams to either side. Jack was just one of several messengers directing both ambulances and civil defence workers to the scene and then staying to help ferry out the wounded.

He reached home, barely able to walk after having had to push his bike for the last mile due to a flat tyre and lacking both the will and the energy to repair it then and there.

Once indoors, he stripped off his uniform and washed away the worst of the smoke and dirt that was adhering to his skin and enmeshed in his hair. Only then did he throw himself down in the chair and close his eyes. Within minutes he was asleep, hardly stirring until he felt a hand on his shoulder shaking him awake.

'Alan Prentiss, Jack, I didn't know if you'd heard.'

'Heard? No, what?' Jack pushed himself upright, reading the concern on his father's face.

'He's in hospital. Injured pretty bad.'

'What happened? He fell, what?'

His father shook his head. 'He wasn't even on duty. Just crossing the road on his way home. Damned blackout – well, you know – it happens all the time. Bastard who hit him, though, never stopped.'

Jack was fully awake now, on his feet.

'Which hospital?'

'Hampstead General.'

'Give us a hand mending this puncture, Dad, will you? I'm going to go see him.'

'Now?'

'Yes, now.'

The nursing sister stopped him at the entrance to the ward. Blue uniform, starched white cuffs and cap. Arms folded across her considerable chest.

'Are you a relative?' she asked, when Jack told her who he had come to see.

'Not really.'

'Not really or not at all?'

'Why does it matter?' he asked, exasperated.

'It matters because only relatives – and close relatives at that – are allowed on to the ward outside visiting hours.'

'And when are they?'

'Two-thirty to three-thirty in the afternoons, six o'clock to seven-thirty in the evenings.'

'That's hopeless.'

'I'm sorry, you'll have to come back tomorrow.'

'But, I can't.'

'Then I'm sorry . . .'

'I have to see him now.'

The sister recrossed her arms. 'Please leave.'

Jack feinted right, then left and tried to dart past. A hand seized him by the collar and hauled him back.

'Young man. You have two alternatives: either go now of your own accord or I shall call for assistance to have you escorted from the premises. In which case there will be no further opportunity for you to visit Mr Prentiss while he is a patient in this hospital. Do I make myself clear?'

'Yes,' Jack mumbled.

'I'm sorry?'

'Yes,' he shouted.

Nonplussed, the sister stood her ground.

Head down, Jack turned and walked away, out through the double doors to the stairway by the lift. When the lift arrived he rode it down to the ground floor, left by the main exit, walked up and down Pond Street twice, went back in and this time took the stairs.

At the far end of the corridor the doors to the ward were unguarded. The sister was nowhere to be seen. Jack made his way quietly along and looked through the glass. Two lines of beds; patients, a few of them, sitting up, most lying down. Not a nurse in sight.

Cautiously, Jack slipped inside. Alan Prentiss was at the far end of the ward, his bed close against a high window looking down over the delivery bay at the rear of building.

Jack ducked down low between the bed and the wall, and, as if suddenly aware someone was there, Prentiss opened his eyes.

'Shh,' Jack whispered, putting a finger to his lips. 'I'm not here.'

'I can see that,' Prentiss whispered back and smiled.

'How are you?'

'For someone with six broken ribs, a fractured pelvis and a broken collarbone, surprisingly okay.'

'What happened?'

Prentiss tried to shrug, but winced sharply instead. 'One minute I was making my way across Holloway Road, the next this car hit me and I was flat on my face in the middle of the road and the car just kept on going. Fortunately, there were several other people around . . .'

'They saw what happened?'

'Maybe. Partly, anyway. The good thing was, they lifted me out of the way before anyone else could run into me, called an ambulance and, well, here I am.'

'But what did they say, whoever it was that saw you get knocked down.'

'They said – two of them, two of the three – they said it looked as if the car had come straight for me almost on purpose. And then accelerated away.'

'But why would anyone do that?'

Before Prentiss could answer, Jack ducked down even lower as a young nurse, wearing mostly white, came into the ward and went to the first bed on the opposite side.

Prentiss leaned towards him, groaning a little at the effort involved. 'All this time I've been documenting the activities of the Fire Brigade, I've had this other little job on the side. For the Robbery Squad, Scotland Yard. Trying to get photographic evidence of Black Market activity, gang involvement, corruption, serious crime. I think maybe someone found out. Got suspicious, at least. Thought I was getting too close.'

Jack could only stare at him, open-mouthed.

The nurse was now several beds nearer, checking temperatures, making notes on a chart clipped to the end of each bed.

Prentiss moved his head even closer.

'Jack, I want you to do me a favour. I wouldn't ask

you, but right now I'm not sure who I can trust. I want you to go to my flat, right? You remember where it is?'

Jack nodded.

'Okay. There's keys in this locker, beside the bed. Take them and let yourself in, grab anything you can find. Prints, rolls of exposed film. There might be some negatives still drying, I'm not sure. Just take a case along, a bag, it doesn't matter what. Something to carry stuff away in.'

'And bring it here?'

'No, not here.'

'The police, then? I could take it to the police station in Kentish Town?'

'No, not there either.' Painful as it was, he swivelled slowly round in the bed. 'A notebook and pencil, Jack, there with the key. Pass them to me.'

The nurse was more than halfway down the ward but still with her back mostly turned away. Higher up, back towards the doors, someone was calling out, trying to get her attention. 'A bedpan, nurse, please. It's urgent!'

Prentiss wrote a name and number down in the book and tore out the page.

'Take it to this person, Jack. At Scotland Yard. New Scotland Yard, really. You know where it is?'

Jack nodded.

'Okay, good. Anything you find, take it to this man.

If you get the chance, phone in advance. Use my name.'

'All right.'

Jack folded the piece of paper and pushed it down into one of his trouser pockets, slipped the keys into the other.

'Good luck, Jack.' With a grimace, Prentiss lowered himself back down.

'Excuse me,' the nurse called, seeing Jack suddenly walking down the centre of the ward. 'Excuse me, but just what do you think you're doing?'

If he heard her, Jack gave no sign.

THIRTY-TWO

It was too much for Jack to keep to himself. Close to overwhelming. And he knew full well that if he told his dad – which he'd been tempted to do – he would never be allowed to follow Alan Prentiss' instructions.

Lilith was using cardboard for a makeshift repair to the sole of one of her shoes when Jack knocked and made his way down into the cellar.

She listened, intrigued, while Jack retold Prentiss' story.

'And, Jack, you believe all of this, yes? You don't think some of this is in his head, his imagination?'

'No, I don't.'

Lilith's face creased with the beginnings of a smile. 'Then wait, please, while I finish with this shoe.'

'You're sure? Sure you want to come? It may be dangerous.'

'Of course. And besides, why else did you come here if not to ask me to be your – what is the expression? – right-hand man?'

The door to the flat was splintered across and it took only seconds to see that the interior had been well and truly trashed. Furniture upended; books and records strewn across the room. The front of the wireless kicked in. The gramophone smashed. In the bedroom, the mattress had been hauled to the floor and gutted, stuffing spread out across the rug; the bed itself had been turned on its side and pushed back against the wall. Jars and saucepans littered the kitchen floor.

Unlike the rest of the flat, the bathroom that Prentiss used as his dark room had every appearance of being searched more methodically. The planks of wood had been removed from across the bath and stacked up against the wall; trays upended into the bath itself. Boxes of photo paper seemed to have been taken carefully from the shelves at the bath end and riffled through, then pushed back into place. Of finished prints there was no sign: all had gone. Negatives, too.

'I think this is what they were really interested in,' Lilith said. 'Where they searched first. Then, when they couldn't find whatever it was they wanted, they lost their tempers and went crazy.'

Jack knelt for a moment amongst the records that lay scattered across the living room floor. Amongst them was the one that had been playing when he'd first come round. Louis Armstrong and his Orchestra. 'St Louis Blues'. Barely damaged, save for a hairline crack across the surface.

'Jack,' Lilith said suddenly, 'what's that over there?'

Just visible, half an inch of something shiny and black was poking out from beneath the upturned settee.

Taking the end carefully between finger and thumb, Lilith eased it out.

It was a short strip of negative film, just five frames in all.

'Here, Jack. Look.'

Taking it across to the window and holding it up to the light, Jack could just make out two figures in outline, the same figures he thought, at a different angle in each of the first four frames, the fifth a blank, more or less solid black.

'What do you think, Jack? What do you think they are up to?'

'Difficult to tell. I suppose they could just be shaking hands . . . '

'I don't think so. Look, Jack. Look again. The one on the left. Isn't he giving the other one something? A small parcel of some kind?'

'I don't know. But there's one way to find out for sure. I just hope I can remember everything Alan showed me.

In the bathroom, Jack paused long enough to picture the dark room set up as it had been. Then, with Lilith watching, he began to restore it piece by piece: first the planks of wood and then the trays, into which he carefully poured the different chemicals. After checking the enlarger was still working, he readied the photo paper and set the negative in place.

'Can you count for me?' he asked.

'I suppose.'

'Okay. But do it like this – one a-thousand, two a-thousand – and don't stop till you reach thirty.'

He switched on and held his breath.

The instant Lilith reached thirty he slid the photo paper out from the enlarger and into the developer.

More counting.

The stop bath next and then the fixer, the image gradually taking shape before his eyes.

A shape Jack thought he recognized.

Lifting the print out carefully with wooden tongs, he held it for several seconds beneath running water before bringing it back to eye level.

After which there was no room for doubt.

THIRTY-THREE

New Scotland Yard was on the Victoria Embankment, not so far from the Houses of Parliament on the north side of the Thames. As Alan Prentiss had suggested, Jack had called ahead, pushing penny after penny into the black box inside the telephone kiosk by Tufnell Park station as he had waited to be put through.

When he arrived, wearing his messenger's uniform, the officer at the entrance was expecting him, passing him on swiftly to a second man who escorted him to the lift and, once Jack was inside, pressed the button for the fifth floor.

'Someone will meet you,' he assured him.

That someone, Jack was surprised to see, was a woman around his mother's age, not in uniform but dressed in civilian clothes.

'Jack Riley?' she asked, with a smile.

'Yes.'

'Come with me. The detective superintendent's expecting you.'

He followed her along the corridor, past door after closed door, until they arrived almost at the end.

'Here we are,' she said.

There was just time for Jack to read the name and rank painted on the door – Detective Superintendent Matthew Fleming – before she knocked and, almost in the same movement, eased the door open.

'Here's the boy, sir.'

'Thank you, Marjorie.'

With a quick smile at Jack, she motioned for him to go inside then closed the door quietly but firmly at his back.

'Jack, good to see you.'

A tall man, taller than Jack's father by a good inch or so, hair turning silvery grey, the superintendent came out from behind his desk, stooping a little as he held out his hand.

'Found your way here without any difficulty?'

Jack nodded and shook the proffered hand.

'Biked it?'

'Yes, sir.'

'Well, let's hope no one steals it from outside.'

Jack understood this for a joke and smiled.

'Take a seat, Jack. Then let's have a look at what you've brought with you.'

Jack took the four photographs he had printed from inside his jacket and placed them on the desk: they showed the same two men standing in front of a partly demolished building; in one photo they were in close conversation, heads together; in another, laughing; in the last two, smiling and shaking hands.

Fleming scanned them all quickly before scrutinizing each one more carefully and setting it back down.

'You don't have any idea who these people are, I suppose, Jack?'

'Yes, sir,' Jack said. 'Yes, sir. I think I do.'

'Do you indeed?'

'Yes, sir.'

Fleming steepled his fingers. 'Then suppose you tell me.'

Jack pointed to the figure on the left, wearing a dark overcoat and a trilby hat with a light band around it, the brim pulled slightly down.

'That man there. He's Vincent Crella. At least, I think so.'

'And what, if anything, do you know about him?'

'He's some kind of gangster.'

A smile passed across the police officer's face. 'And

this?' he asked, pointing at the second man, standing there hatless, raincoat collar turned up.

'I . . . think that's . . .' Jack hesitated, glancing up uncertainly.

'Go ahead. Say what you think.'

'I think his name is Reardon.'

'And how do you know him?'

'I've met him, sir. He's a . . . a police officer. A detective sergeant at Kentish Town.'

'That he is.' With a sigh, Fleming pushed a hand up through his hair. 'Anthony Aloysious Reardon. A good copper, Jack. Arrest record, second to none. Ambitious, too. Next in line for promotion. And ambition's no bad thing in a man, eh, Jack? Your dad – he's in the services somewhere I suppose?'

'The Fire Brigade, sir.'

'I see,' smiling, 'like father like son. But your dad now, I expect he'd like to be made up to Leading Fireman, don't you think?'

'Yes, I suppose so. I mean, yes, I'm sure he would.'

'And you, you've ambitions of your own, I dare say?'

'I'm not sure. I . . .'

'Well, all in good time. And Mr Reardon, as I say, has ambitions he works very hard to achieve. Sometimes, perhaps a trifle too hard.'

The superintendent swivelled round in his chair and looked out over the river; swivelled back.

'One of the things about our job, Jack – CID especially – it necessitates spending time in the company of people whose activities we strongly disapprove of. People who, in the normal run of things, we would turn our backs on, cross the street to avoid. Lowlifes. Ne'er do wells. In this case . . .' He gestured towards the photographs. 'Gangsters, as you succinctly put it, such as Mr Vincent Crella. Sometimes it's the only way to obtain the information we need. You understand, Jack?'

'Yes . . . I think so.'

'Good, good.'

'So . . .'

'Yes, Jack?'

'That's what . . . that's what's going on in these photos? Detective Sergeant Reardon is talking to Vincent Crella to find out what he knows?'

'Smart lad, Jack. Exactly that.'

'Then why . . .?'

'Go on.'

'No, it doesn't matter.'

'Go ahead, Jack. If there's something troubling you, ask while you have the chance.'

Jack wriggled a little on his seat. 'It's just that if that's all that's going on, and if, as you say, it's the kind of thing that happens all the time, why are these photographs so important?'

The superintendent squeezed out a smile. 'A good question, Jack. In response to which, I'll say two things. Firstly, we have no way of knowing for certain if it was these particular photographs whoever searched Alan Prentiss' flat was after. I'm sure there were many more. And secondly, whereas we might understand DS Reardon's presence in those pictures illustrates nothing more than a rather unpleasant part of his job, were any of Vincent Crella's colleagues or, indeed, his rivals to see them, they might put a very different interpretation on them. See them as evidence that Crella was becoming over friendly with the enemy. In which case there might be dire consequences where he's concerned.'

'So that's why . . .?'

Fleming cut him off by getting quickly to his feet and holding out his hand.

'It's been a pleasure to meet you, Jack. And thank you once again for your assistance.'

The superintendent's grip was firm and he didn't immediately release Jack's hand. 'Anything that's been said between us today, Jack, anything you've seen, Mum's the word, eh? You'll say nothing to anyone?'

Jack shook his head.

'I have your word on that? Your word of honour?'

'Yes.'

'Not a word to your father?'

'No, sir.'

'Your girlfriend?'

'No.'

Fleming laughed. 'Good lad! And if you visit Alan again in the hospital, Jack, as I'm sure you will, be sure to give him my best wishes for a speedy recovery. Now Marjorie will show you out of the building, make sure you don't get lost.'

As if by some pre-arranged signal, the office door opened and Marjorie was there waiting. His bike was where he'd left it, chained to the railings, safe and sound. He rode home slowly, chewing over what the detective superintendent had said and thinking there must be a great deal more about which he'd said nothing at all.

THIRTY-FOUR

'You made these prints yourself, Jack? From that strip of neg you found in the flat?'

'With my friend Lilith's help, yes.'

Alan Prentiss' expression was one of admiration and disbelief. He was sitting up in bed, propped up against pillows, the second set of prints Jack had made laid out on the white sheet in front of him. Jack had been there since the beginning of official hospital visiting time and there had been nothing the ward sister could do other than fire off a succession of nasty looks in his direction.

'You did well, Jack,' Prentiss said. 'Your first time, especially. This is really good work.'

'I just had to keep remembering what you'd said.

The timings and everything.'

Prentiss nodded. 'The detective super, he doesn't know you made an extra set?'

'No.'

'Maybe just as well.' Prentiss shifted uneasily as a pain shot through him. 'What did he say, anyway, about the photos when you showed him?'

'That Reardon was just doing his job. Getting, you know, information from Crella.'

Prentiss smiled and shook his head.

'You mean it's not true?' Jack said.

'Half-true, at most.'

'What then?'

'I don't know, Jack. Maybe it's best you don't get yourself too involved. I'd hate for you to end up in hospital like me, all because someone thought you knew too much.'

'But I am involved. Already.'

'Very well.' Prentiss looked along to the next bed, where the patient was sleeping fast, untroubled by visitors. 'But what I'm going to tell you . . .'

'I understand.'

'When I was briefed at New Scotland Yard, before taking this assignment with Blue Watch, there were certain things they were interested in. One was gang activity in the area, black market activities especially. Anything involving spirits and cigarettes. Another was any evidence of collusion between those gangs and the local force.'

'And that's what this is?' Jack asked, indicating the photos. 'What did you call it? Collusion?'

'It's what it points to, yes, I think so.'

He broke off as another sharp pain lanced across his chest. Sipped water and resettled before continuing.

'Ever since Vincent Crella came down from north of the border, Scotland Yard's been monitoring his activities as closely as they can. And, from what the detective super told me, the current feeling is that since Crella set up camp in DS Reardon's manor, he and the detective sergeant have got too close. The suspicion being that, while doing his job, excelling at it, in fact, Reardon has obligingly locked up several of Crella's potential rivals in return for, shall we say, certain favours. A share, most likely, of Crella's ill-gotten gains.'

'And those photographs, they're proof?'

'On their own, no. But if the Yard has been building a case against them both for a long time, those prints might just prove to be the icing on the cake.'

'On the case,' Jack said and laughed.

'Yes, that's right. On the case.' But when he joined in with the laughter, it turned into a fit of coughing, which in turn led to a fresh bout of pain and brought the sister over to the bed.

'I think Mr Prentiss has had enough entertainment for one day, young man, don't you?'

Jack scrambled to his feet and reached out for the photographs, but Prentiss stayed his hand.

'I think perhaps it's best to leave these here with me.'

'Can't I take one? It is my first ever effort at printing, after all.'

'All right, fair enough. Just don't go flashing it around. Better still, don't go showing it to anyone.'

Before he could change his mind, Jack picked up the photo of the two men shaking hands and slipped it from sight.

'The negatives, though, Jack. You'd better let me keep hold of those.'

Jack took the envelope containing the strip of negatives from inside his jacket and placed it in Prentiss' hand.

'Thanks, Jack. For everything. And take care.'

'Do my best.'

He set off down the ward.

'And try to keep out of any more trouble,' Prentiss called after him, but if Jack heard him, he gave no sign.

Jack went straight from the hospital to find Lilith, but she was nowhere to be seen. The entrance to the cellar had been securely covered and well disguised, as if, wherever she had gone, she thought she might be there for some time.

When he cycled past the next morning on his way to the station there was still no sign. And in the end it was Lilith who found him.

'Someone to see you, Jack,' Rose called across the yard with a broad grin.

Lilith was sitting astride her bike, wearing a bizarre combination of yellow cycle jacket, a bright red skirt over dark trousers, wellington boots and a blue beret pulled artfully over to one side.

'Aren't you going to introduce us, Jack?' Rose said.

Jack could sense himself going red. He mumbled a reply and ushered Lilith out of the station as swiftly as he could. In the café he ordered two cups of tea and a chelsea bun for them to share.

The café was strangely quiet, but Jack kept his voice low, as he brought Lilith up to date on what he had learned of the two men in the photograph – Reardon and Crella – and the suspicious relationship between them.

'Do you still have the photograph?' Lilith asked.

'One of the prints, yes, why?'

'Let me see it, please.'

Cautiously, Jack slid the photograph across the table.

'This man here,' Lilith said, pointing.

'Crella?'

'I think I know him.'

'What d'you mean?'

'I thought he looked familiar when you first developed the photographs, but I wasn't sure. But now I am. I've seen him, Jack. I know I have.'

'Where?'

'You know the public house on Leverton Street? These last few days the landlady has been finding odd jobs for me. Peeling vegetables, washing glasses. Things like this.'

'And that's where you've seen Crella?'

'Yes. He and the landlady, I think they are friends. Anyway, there is this room upstairs, private. This Crella meets there with some other men.' Lilith shook her head. 'I have seen these men, Jack, and I do not think they are such nice people.'

Jack laughed. 'That's because they're most likely crooks.'

'It is not funny, Jack.'

'I know.'

'Then why do you laugh?'

'I don't know,' Jack said and laughed some more.

They rode back along the main road side by side, the first air raid siren of the evening sounding its shrill alarm as they swung left towards the street where Lilith lived.

'If you do see this Crella again,' Jack said once they'd arrived, 'steer well clear. He's dangerous.'

'It's okay, Jack, you don't have to worry. I'll be careful.'

Looking up, they heard the throb of enemy planes growing ever closer overhead.

'You'd better go, Jack.'

'I know.'

Without thinking, he leaned forward and kissed her, quickly, on the cheek.

'Bye.'

'Bye, Jack.'

Lilith stood watching as he cycled away, gathering speed, then slid the entrance to the cellar aside and climbed down into the dark.

THIRTY-FIVE

The raid that night was one of the closest to where he lived that Jack could remember. The Anderson shelter echoed with reverberation after reverberation, the very ground beneath where Jack lay seeming to rise and shake. It was doubtful he slept for more than thirty or forty minutes continuously, emerging finally before it was properly light and making his way into the house just as the all clear sounded.

If he'd remembered correctly, his father should be coming back off duty that morning, so, after splashing water on his face in the bathroom and cleaning his teeth, he filled the kettle and set it to boil, and sliced bread for toast.

When his father arrived, he brought the acrid smell

of smoke and burning timbers into the house with him. His face, always smirched with soot when he finished a long shift, was almost solid black apart from two curves of pinkish-white above the eyes where his eyebrows had been singed clear away.

'Christ, Jack! What a sodding night!'

'Here, let me help.' Jack assisted him in stripping off his tunic, pulling off his boots.

'Lost a man tonight, Jack,' Ben Riley said, slumping into a chair. 'Young Taylor. Only been with us a matter of weeks. Up on the roof of one of them factories off the Cali. Bugger gave way beneath him. Fell five floors to the bottom, poor bastard, never stood a chance.'

For several long moments, neither of them spoke.

Jack saw to the tea and toast.

His father lit a cigarette.

'Everyone else get through okay?' Jack asked.

'Yes, pretty much.'

'Charlie?'

His father looked up. 'Charlie's all right. Why d'you ask?'

Jack shrugged. 'Since that business with the watch, the one you thought might've been stolen, you've never mentioned him, that's all. You used to talk about him all the time.'

Ben Riley sat forward in his chair. 'He's not spoken of it again. Not to me nor, far as I know, anyone else.

So I've said nothing either.' He picked up his cup. 'Let sleeping dogs lie.'

'But you're still friends?'

'Yes, of course. Just not . . . well, not quite in the same way as before.'

His father fast asleep the moment his head touched the pillow, Jack finished getting himself ready, checking the air in his tyres and adjusting his brakes, before setting off for the station. Rose and Bobbie were waiting to ambush him the moment he arrived.

'Who was that girl?' Rose wanted to know.

'Come on, Jack,' Bobbie said, 'you crafty young devil. Who is she?'

Jack tried to push his way past, but they hemmed him in.

'You've been keeping that quiet,' Rose said. 'Sly thing, you.'

Jack tried again, but Rose simply caught hold of his arm and hauled him back.

'You know what they say about the quiet ones, Bobbie?'

'No, what's that, Rose?'

'It's always them that's up to something when you'd least expect it.'

Jack pulled himself free. 'She's a friend and that's all.'

'And my name's Winston Churchill,' said Bobbie, with a smirk.

'And I'm the Queen,' laughed Rose.

'Come on, Jack,' Bobbie urged. 'Don't be so mean. At least, tell us her name.'

'Lilith.'

'Say again?'

'Lilith.'

'That's a lovely name,' Rose said. 'Unusual. A lovely name.'

'She's a lovely girl,' said Bobbie.

'Beautiful,' said Rose.

'You're a lucky boy, Jack,' Bobbie said and, before he could step aside, gave him a quick hug. 'A lucky lad.'

Yes, she is beautiful, Jack thought, as he went inside to check his duties for the day. She really is.

'What are you grinning at?' the despatcher said, looking up from his desk.

'Nothing, sir. Nothing at all.'

But the same grin kept returning, off and on, throughout the day.

When he arrived home, eight hours later, there was a note from Lilith sticking out from underneath his front door.

Jack: Come round as soon as you can. Urgent!
Lilith xx

Stopping only to change out of his sweaty uniform, and having spent more than enough time in the saddle for one day, he decided to walk. Lilith was waiting for him in the cellar, the words tumbling out of her mouth before Jack had finished descending the makeshift ladder.

'I saw him, Jack, I saw him today at the pub. Crella. He was there this afternoon, in that upstairs room. The landlady told me to take up a tray of sandwiches. And Jack, Jack, guess what? The other man, he was there too.'

'The other . . .'

'The other man from the photograph, the policeman.'

'Reardon?'

'Yes.'

Jack sat down. Lilith's face was animated, alive.

'What happened?' Jack asked.

'Nothing, really. Not at first. I knocked on the door as the landlady had told me. I could hear them talking inside but as soon as I knocked they stopped and someone shouted to come in. I walked into the room, set the tray down on the table, turned around and came back out.'

'And Reardon was there? You're sure?'

'Yes. Along with the man Crella and three others.'

'You didn't hear what they were saying?'

'Not then. But when I went out, instead of closing the door properly, I only pulled it to. And waited at the top of the stairs.'

'Go on . . .'

'One of them noticed the door, of course. Said something about "stupid girl" and slammed it shut.'

'So you didn't really . . .'

Lilith was beaming. 'Yes, Jack. Yes, I did. Before they closed the door, I heard what one of them was saying. Crella I think it was, though I can't be sure. "Gilbey's," he said. "Gilbey's. First thing tomorrow." And then one of the others said, "Okay, I'll make sure the coast's kept clear."'

'That would be Reardon,' Jack said.

'I don't know, Jack. But Gilbey's, what is that?'

'A wine merchant's and distillery. In Camden. It's huge. There was a trip round there from school. I didn't go but I remember the older kids talking about maybe getting a job there when they left. They must employ hundreds. There's not just one building but several, with tunnels underneath joining them together. And every morning, there's this train that takes stuff down to the docks. Lorries, too. Loaded up with all kinds of wine and whisky and everything.'

'And you think these men, this gang, they are planning to rob one of these lorries?'

Jack nodded. 'That's exactly what I think they're planning to do.'

'We must tell the police.'

'Yes, but which police? Report it to the wrong ones and there's a danger that Reardon will get to hear of it, in which case they'll call it off. Change their plan.'

'So what can we do?'

'Forget about the local police. Go straight to Scotland Yard.'

'Can we do that?'

'I think so.'

Lilith rubbed her hands together. 'Jack, it's exciting.'

He nodded agreement. 'When you heard them talking, they didn't mention a particular time, just first thing?'

'That's all. First thing tomorrow.'

'In that case, we'd better get there good and early.'

'But Jack . . .'

'How else are we going to see what happens? I wouldn't miss it for anything, would you?'

THIRTY-SIX

Six o'clock.

Six thirty.

When exactly was 'early'? Sunrise, officially, was not for another hour.

Jack and Lilith crouched, out of sight, on the narrow steps leading up to Oval Road from the canal, the darkness around them only slowly beginning to fade. From somewhere deep in the heart of the city came the sound of sirens sounding the all clear.

'The police,' Lilith whispered, 'why aren't they here?'

'For all we know, they might be here already.'

'You think so?'

'They're not going to want the gang to see them,

are they? Not if they can catch them in the act.'

Lilith fell quiet, thoughtful.

A rat scuttled by on the towpath below.

'You did tell them? The time and everything?'

'Yes,' Jack said. It wasn't like Lilith to be nervous and he wasn't sure why.

He hadn't spoken to Matthew Fleming directly, but Marjorie had remembered him from his visit and promised she would pass on the message to the detective superintendent without fail.

Another ten minutes passed.

Twenty . . .

'I'm sorry, Jack,' Lilith said quietly. 'Perhaps I got it wrong. Perhaps it wasn't today at all.'

But then they heard it, the sound of a heavy lorry coming towards them from the far end of Oval Road.

Lilith squeezed Jack's arm.

Closer, it was just possible to make out the name, *W & A Gilbey*, painted on the side.

The lorry was just drawing level with Jamestown Road when, with a roar of acceleration, a black saloon came out of the turning fast and swung across into the lorry's path, forcing it to judder to a halt.

Four men, masks over their faces, jumped from the car, weapons in their hands – iron bars, a length of timber, a shotgun – and ran, two and two, to either side of the driver's cab.

'Get down! Get down!'

One of the iron bars swung high and crashed against the cab window hard. Shouts of alarm and the sound of breaking glass.

'I said get bloody down!'

A second blow, to the windscreen this time, splintering it across.

'Get down from there or else!' Even though he was wearing a mask, and without his trademark hat, Jack recognized Vincent Crella as the man who was now holding the shotgun menacingly raised.

'Jack,' Lilith said, 'what can we do?'

'Nothing. There's nothing we can do.'

'Where are the police?'

'I don't know.'

One of the men wrenched the cab door open and, reluctantly, the driver climbed down, his mate following suit at the other side.

'Turn around,' Crella said, and, reversing the weapon smartly, he struck the driver full force on the back of the head.

Lilith gasped.

'Let's go,' Crella said, stepping over the driver's fallen body, one hand reaching up towards the cab door.

Two of the gang climbed into the cab with him, the third one hurrying back to the car they'd arrived in.

'Jack, they're getting away.'

With a crunching of gears the lorry began to move and as it did so the first of the police cars that had been waiting out of sight came fast along Oval Road towards them, bells ringing, lights flashing, a second car following in its wake. A third car approached fast from the opposite direction, blocking any possible retreat.

The lorry lurched to a halt and the men jumped down, scattered and ran, two of them down towards the canal where more police were already waiting.

The driver of the black saloon was revving its engine hard, anxious to make a getaway, and Crella jumped on to the running board, clinging on to the dashboard with one arm through the open window, the shotgun still tight in his other hand, as the car sped off with a squeal of tyres.

One of the police cars moved to intercept it and, as Jack and Lilith watched, open-mouthed, the getaway car swerved, spun out of control and skidded into a brick wall on the far side of the road.

Leaping clear, Crella took to his heels. Running back towards the canal, he vaulted the low fence alongside the steps and scrambled down on to the canal path, near where Jack and Lilith were standing.

'Stay here,' Jack said.

'Don't,' Lilith warned, but too late. He was off in close pursuit.

At first Crella seemed to be pulling away, but after a hundred yards or so he had slowed sufficiently for Jack to be gaining ground.

A police car sped past them along the road, heading for the junction ahead, a bridge across the road, the next set of steps.

Jack was now no more than a dozen yards behind and gaining.

A few yards more and he sprang, catching hold of Crella's right leg and bringing him crashing down, the shotgun jarring out of his grasp and toppling into the waters of the canal.

Swivelling fast, Crella kicked out with his other leg and struck Jack in the face, high above the left eye, raising blood; kicked again and drove his heel into Jack's shoulder, once, twice.

Despite the pain he was feeling, Jack held on for all he was worth. Behind them, back along the canal, the shrill sound of police whistles, louder and louder. Men running. From ahead now, as well as behind.

As they grappled on the canal path, Crella's elbow caught Jack in the face and then a boot drove hard into his inner thigh and, with a shout of pain, he let go.

Crella scrambled to his feet and started to run, heading for the steps no more than twenty yards ahead.

Twenty. Fifteen. Ten.

Jack watched, still doubled over in pain, as two

burly policemen appeared at the foot of the steps, Crella unable to stop before rushing smack into them. One seized his right arm, the other his left, and, between them, they spun him round, forced his arms together and clicked handcuffs tight around his wrists.

'You all right, son?'

One of the officers who had been in pursuit along the canal path, seeing that Crella was safely in custody, bent over Jack and started helping him to his feet.

'Nasty knock on the head there,' the officer said. 'Might need to get you off to casualty.'

'No, it's okay,' Jack said. 'I'm fine.' And promptly lost consciousness and collapsed into the policeman's arms.

THIRTY-SEVEN

Jack came to in the ambulance, not knowing quite where he was, voices around him drifting in and out. When he went to raise a hand towards where his head was hurting, someone – he couldn't see who – took hold of his arm, firmly but gently, and lowered it back down.

Without meaning to, he closed his eyes and fell back to sleep.

When he awoke he was in a hospital bed, bandage round his head and his father, in full uniform, was sitting alongside him.

'Welcome back to the living,' Ben Riley said with a laugh.

'What . . . what happened?'

'Don't you remember?'

'Not really. I mean, yes, I was chasing after Crella, along the canal. And then . . .' Jack started to shake his head but quickly thought better of it. 'After that, I'm not sure.'

'He must have caught you one with the heel of his boot, by the look of things. Once if not twice. You lost a lot of blood. Passed out cold.'

'But Crella, they got him all right, didn't they?'

'Red-handed, thanks to you. You and young Lilith.'

'Where is she?'

'Talking to the police, a detective superintendent . . .'

'Fleming.'

'That's it. Telling them what she knows. She'll be along to see you once she's done.'

Before Ben Riley could say anything more, a white-coated doctor arrived, stethoscope poking from his pocket, X-ray in hand, and perched near the end of Jack's bed.

'Well, young man. From the look of this . . .' Holding up the X-ray. '. . . you've had a lucky escape. No concussion. No haemorrhaging. Nothing worse than a small fracture which, all being well, will heal with time. It could have been a whole lot worse.'

'And no after effects, doctor?' Ben Riley asked.

'Not as long as he's sensible. Keeps away from dangerous criminals; doesn't go charging head first into any brick walls.'

'Can I go home, then?' Jack asked.

'We'll keep you in overnight, I think. As a precaution. Nothing untoward, you can be on your way first thing.'

'Thank you, doctor,' Ben Riley said and shook the doctor's hand.

Next to visit was Lilith, at which point Jack's dad made himself scarce and gave them some time to themselves.

'So Jack, you will survive, I think?' She reached for his hand and he didn't pull it away. 'You are a little too . . . I think the word is foolhardy.'

Jack grinned. 'What else was I going to do? I couldn't just stand there and watch them get away.'

'Just as well for us you didn't,' said a voice from the doorway.

Detective Superintendent Fleming stepped forward, rather self-consciously carrying a bunch of grapes.

'Jack, we owe you – you and your friend here – a considerable debt of gratitude. Not simply for foiling a hijack that, if successful, would have seen the robbers getting away with some £4,000 worth of wines and spirits, but for delivering, as it were, Vincent Crella and three of his gang into our hands. If the courts do their job, Crella will go down for a very long time.'

'And what about Reardon?' Jack asked. 'From what Lilith saw, he must have been in on it, too.'

'Detective Sergeant Reardon – in a phrase he will have used himself many times – is currently helping the police with their enquiries.'

Fleming held out his hand.

'I'm not one to advocate the public taking the law into their own hands, especially where armed robbery is concerned, but having said that, what you did, Jack Riley, was brave above and beyond the call of duty.'

'Thank you, sir.'

'And you, young lady,' Fleming said, shaking Lilith's hand in turn, 'were every bit as brave, I'm sure.'

'Look, Jack,' Lilith said when the detective superintendent had gone. 'Look there.' She was pointing through the window at the end of the ward. 'You see that, bright and clear, it is what they call a Bomber's Moon.'

Jack looked out past her head and shoulders to where a white semicircle sat like a cut-out in the sky.

'Makes it too easy for the Germans to see their targets,' Jack said. 'It's not a good sign.'

As he spoke, the brittle rattle of nearby ack-ack guns volleyed upwards, seeking out their targets.

'There are more enemy planes than guns, Jack. Some always get through. One at least. We must hope its bombs do not fall on us.'

For a moment she rested her hand again on his.

'Try to sleep now, Jack. Get well.'

Long after she had gone, Jack lay back in his bed, the sounds of the ward rising and falling around him, staring through the window at the moon, framed like a painting in a square of glass.

THIRTY-EIGHT

After a frustratingly long wait before the doctor gave the okay for him to be officially discharged, Jack finally arrived home, mid-afternoon, to find a postcard from his mother on the mantelpiece in the front room and a note from his father resting up against the bread bin in the kitchen.

The postcard had a picture on the front of a ploughed field and some trees; a couple of forlorn-looking sheep. Her writing on the reverse was small and neat in blue-black ink.

More heroics!
Well and bravely done, but please take care!!
Thinking of you. Lots of love, Mum xxx

No matter how hard he tried, the postmark was too blurred and indistinct for him to be able to read.

His father's message was more down to earth.

Have restocked with food as best I can.
Take it easy and keep off your bike. Dad x

Jack checked the cupboard: beans and pilchards; pilchards and beans. Cornflakes. Marmite. Jam. There was a small loaf of bread in the bin, a fresh pint of milk in the larder. Two apples. Half-a-dozen eggs.

He took one of the apples into the front room and flicked through the pages of the paper.

Their majesties the King and Queen today visited
Merseyside where they inspected air raid damage
and casualties, chatted to victims, first aid parties
and ARP personnel . . .

Thirteen Italian 'planes and twelve German
'planes were shot down by the RAF yesterday.
Two British fighters were lost. Seven of the Italians
were destroyed while trying to attack shipping off
the Thames Estuary . . .

Retail coal prices may go up by 1d. per cwt. as

the result of an increase of 1s. 6d. per ton in pit-head prices authorized last night . . .

Jack let the newspaper slip through his fingers and yawned. Not once but twice; not twice, but several times. One of the last things the doctor had done was to warn him that he might find himself feeling more tired that usual.

'Don't fight it, young man, whatever you do. It's your body's way of telling you to get as much rest as you can and give that noggin of yours a chance to heal.'

Jack had had it in mind to walk down and see if Lilith was around, spend some time with her before the inevitable evening raid, but try as he might he couldn't stop his eyes from closing.

When he awoke it was dark.

For a few seconds he didn't know what had woken him and then he did. The urgent wail of sirens and then what seemed like explosion after explosion, the first of them near enough to rattle the windows in their frames, the second and third further off yet not so far. North and west, Jack thought, beyond the railway bridge, towards the Fields.

Towards where Lilith lived.

Quickly, he pulled on his coat and shoes. Walking fast, he could see the smoke from the explosions rising through the dark air. At the end of Lilith's street he started to run. Each time his foot pounded down on the pavement it sent a small shockwave of pain through his head, but he didn't care. The shell-like walls that, up to now, had remained standing either side of Lilith's cellar had disappeared. In their place were jagged piles, more than six feet high, of broken brick and masonry that had fallen across the cellar entrance, hiding it completely.

Jack scrambled over the wreckage, feet slipping beneath him, calling Lilith's name, the words swallowed almost as soon as they were uttered by the dust-and-smoke-filled air.

Tears sprang to his eyes and, angrily, he wiped them away with his sleeve.

Think, he told himself. Think!

The nearest ARP post was back by Tufnell Park tube station, the way he'd come. Five minutes away, at most. Three, if he ran. Maxie Freeman was there, calmly rolling a cigarette, when Jack arrived.

'This friend of yours,' Freeman asked, 'you're sure she would have been down there? This cellar?'

'I think so, yes.'

'But you can't be certain?'

'No, but I can't think where else she could have been. Not after dark. With the sirens, especially.'

'All right. I'll do what I can. There's a salvage team over at Churchill. I'll see if I can't pull a few away from there. Best you get back down and wait. And try not to worry. I'll have someone along as soon as I can.'

Jack did as Freeman suggested. He began moving debris away, brick by broken brick, aware of the near-futility of what he was doing; all the while unable to shake the memory of seeing Lilith at the place where her aunt and sister had died, hearing her voice in some small space, deep inside his head.

. . . ever since then, I have felt guilty to be still alive.

When the salvage team arrived there were five of them, dressed in dark overalls, all volunteers, their leader a tall man with strong Welsh accent and broken nose.

'Enoch,' he said, introducing himself. 'And you're Jack?'

Briskly, they shook hands.

'If this young lady's down there like you say, we'll get her out, I promise you that.'

What he didn't say, but Jack understood, was that if Lilith had been in the cellar when the bomb had landed and the walls had caved in, there was no knowing how badly injured she might be. No way of knowing if she were still alive.

The men set to work methodically, armed with long-handled shovels, pickaxes and their bare hands. Layer after layer was lifted away, exposing even more broken brick, even more splintered timber than before.

When Jack, unable to stand frustratedly by, piled in to help, Enoch counselled patience: 'Watch what we're doing, take your rhythm from us. No offence, but we're the experts, see?'

Jack choked back a response and did as he was told.

And, amazingly, the pile, which had been at least head high when they started, had now come down to a more manageable level, though it was still too deep and wide for Jack's peace of mind. Bending forward, hard to the task, he was only vaguely aware of vehicles pulling up on the tarmac behind.

'Need a little help here?'

He spun round at the sound of his father's voice.

Ben Riley stood at the pavement's edge, half a dozen other firemen alongside, all of their faces smeared with smoke and dust.

'Just on our way back to the station and realized what was going on. Thought we might stop off and lend a hand.'

'Welcome,' Enoch said. 'Only, like I told our young friend here, slow but steady wins the race.'

'Fair enough,' Ben Riley said. 'Charlie, the rest of you lads, let's get to work.'

And get to work they did: the extra manpower making all the difference. Three feet deep of rubble rapidly became two, became one, became – almost – none.

'There, look!' Jack shouted. 'There's the way in.'

Carefully, they lifted clear the old door that had lain

across the cellar entrance, a few loose pieces of brick falling in and bouncing off the cellar steps.

Jack shouted Lilith's name. Shouted once and once again, the words echoing down into the darkness.

'Quiet,' his father said. 'Listen.'

Weak and barely audible, from the depths of the cellar, came a faint reply.

'Here,' his father said, handing Jack his torch. 'Take this and down you go.'

Part of the floor above had caved in during the blast. Everything was covered in a thick coating of dust and fallen brick.

'Jack? Jack, is that you?'

At first he couldn't see her, but then there she was: her face pale in the torchlight, paler than usual, her hair stuck to one side of her scalp and dark with blood.

Something inside Jack trembled and shook.

'Jack,' Lilith said, trying for a smile, 'you might have come a little sooner, I think.'

She took one wavering step forward and collapsed into his arms. Holding her steady against his body, Jack called back over his shoulder for help. His father was the first to respond and, carefully, they lifted her, barely conscious, out into the air.

An ambulance was on its way.

'We'd best be getting on,' his father said. 'You go with her to the hospital, make sure she's all right. If they're not going to keep her in, you could bring her back to our place. For now at least. Unless you've got a better idea.'

In the ambulance, Lilith opened her eyes just once, saw Jack sitting beside her holding her hand, and smiled. 'What do you say, Jack, we could have matching bandages, do you think?'

Before he could answer, her eyes had closed, her hand warm inside his. The hospital entrance just ahead.

'It's you again, is it?' the casualty nurse said, recognizing Jack as he stepped down from the ambulance.

'And who's this?' she said, easing the stretcher on to a trolley. 'Your girlfriend, I suppose?'

'No,' Jack said, then corrected himself almost immediately. 'Yes. Yes, she is.'

'Good for you,' the nurse said and winked. 'Now why don't you get yourself off to the canteen while we see to this young lady here. Sooner we do that, the sooner we'll have her fit to get back to you, all patched up and looking like new. How does that sound?'

Jack thought it sounded pretty good: pretty good, indeed.

He waited until the trolley had disappeared from sight through the double doors, then turned away. Somewhere in the distance a siren was sounding the all clear and in less than eight hours the sun would be rising on another day.

END NOTES

My own memories of the Second World War are distant and unclear. There was an Anderson shelter in the garden – still in place years later, covered over with earth and grass – but I have no recollection of having used it, though I suppose I must have. I do have some memory, however, of sheltering in the space under the stairs, along with our neighbours from the flat above.

More clearly, I remember being in my great-aunts' flat in Brighton when a bomb exploded close enough to send all the pots and pans flying from the shelves to the kitchen floor. And, I remember more vividly, on the same visit, when my mother and I were walking along the seafront, an enemy plane came over low, strafing the promenade with machine gun fire, and a man pushed us under one of the benches for shelter.

My other abiding memory, less traumatic, is of my father, tall in his Auxiliary Fireman's uniform, standing in the living room of our basement flat alongside several of his colleagues, having called in on their way back to the station for a cup of tea.

This book, as much as anything, is for him.

For details of life in London during the Blitz, I used four major sources, Tom Harrison's *Living Through the Blitz* (Collins, 1976), Juliet Gardner's *Wartime Britain 1939-1945* (Headline, 2004), the same author's *The Blitz: The British Under Attack* (Harper Press, 2010) and Philip Ziegler's *London at War 1939-1945* (Pimlico, 2002).

For information about the work of the London Fire Brigade and Auxiliary Fire Service during the period, three books were especially helpful: *Firemen at War* by Neil Wallington (Jeremy Mills, 2005), *Firefighters and the Blitz* by Francis Beckett (Merlin Press, 2010) and *Fire and Water: The London Firefighters' Blitz 1940-42 Remembered* (Jeremy Mills, 2005), an anthology of accounts and stories written by fire officers themselves and first published in August 1942 to mark the creation of the National Fire Service.

Two films were also of great use, both from 1943, and both available on DVD: the documentary *Fires*

Were Started, by Humphrey Jennings (1943) and *The Bells Go Down*, a fictional snapshot of life in the AFS during the Blitz.

There are also two very interesting websites, www.wwiifire.co.uk, which is run by the World War 2 Fire Services Living History Group and www.london-fire.gov.uk, the site of the London Fire Brigade.

For details of criminal activity in London during the Blitz, including mention of Billy Hill and the Kentish Town Gang, I'm indebted to Donald Thomas's highly readable *An Underworld At War* (John Murray, 2004). And to find out more about the top secret work Jack's mum was involved in at Bletchley Park, there are a number of books available, including *The Secret Life of Bletchley Park* by Sinclair McKay and *Enigma* by Robert Harris, or you could log on at http://www.bletchleypark.org.uk/content/hist/history.rhtm

And finally to stress that this is a work of fiction and, as such, places have been changed where necessary, streets and incidents relocated, and characters invented, while leaving – hopefully – the basic framework of this period of our history – and the work of the Auxiliary Fire Service – intact.

John Harvey, London, June 2012, December 2015 and January 2019

ABOUT THE AUTHOR

JOHN HARVEY taught English and Drama in various secondary schools before turning to writing. Best known for his crime fiction – notably the Nottingham-based Charlie Resnick series – he is also a poet and dramatist, having worked on scripts for TV, radio and the theatre. After living in Nottingham for a good many years, he now lives in north London, where he was born and grew up and where this book is set.

The recipient of Honorary Doctorates from the Universities of Nottingham and Hertfordshire, in 2007 he was awarded the Crime Writers' Association's highest honour, the Diamond Dagger.